Year
of the
Drought

Year
of the
Drought

ROLAND BUTI

TRANSLATED BY CHARLOTTE MANDELL

THIS TRANSLATION WAS PREPARED WITH THE SUPPORT OF

prohelvetia

First published in Great Britain in 2017 by Old Street Publishing Ltd
Yowlestone House, Tiverton, Devon EX16 8LN
www.oldstreetpublishing.co.uk

ISBN 978-1-910400-37-1

10 9 8 7 6 5 4 3 2 1

A CIP catalogue record for this title is available from the British Library.

Printed and bound in the United Kingdom by
CPI Group (UK) Ltd, Croydon CR0 4YY

To my parents

Year
of the
Drought

"Every sunny day that goes by is another step towards catastrophe."

A spokesperson for the Ministry of Agriculture, June 26, 1976.

It was the month of June, in the year 1976. I was thirteen. It was the start of the summer holidays. It was the year of the drought.

Tankers were bringing water from the lakes to the villages. Beneath a sky as yellow as corn, soldiers with their trucks and engine pumps were trying to save whatever crops could still be saved. The government had activated its emergency plan.

It hadn't rained in weeks. It hadn't snowed in the mountains during the winter, either, so the water table hadn't risen in the spring. Everything below was dry, everything on the surface was dry, and our land looked like a hard, stale cracker. Some said the sun had suddenly moved closer to the earth; others that the earth had shifted its axis and drawn nearer to the sun. I myself was of the opinion that an asteroid had fallen somewhere in the area, a huge heavenly body composed of an unknown metal, and giving off invisible toxic vapours. What explanation could there be, other than gases spreading slowly towards the village and poisoning us all without our realising it, insidiously transforming my mother into another person, making us all lose control of our lives during that summer, and bringing an end to my childhood?

For days, Rudy had been telling me that the grass smelled bad. When I asked him why, he replied, sadly and seriously, that it was suffering. This was just like Rudy, to imagine that vegetable matter could manifest its discomfort by giving off a malodorous sweat. A stench of celery and sulphur floated in the air of our back garden, above its scattered tufts of sickly grass trampled by cattle. The ivy that clung to the kitchen garden wall had turned almost black. The sun heated the stone, crumpled the leaves and twisted its shrivelled stems as they made one last effort not to break off from their branches and fall to the sandy ground. When I examined the plant's tendrils, they looked like tiny fists squeezed in despair. I had to admit that everything stank.

My favourite hiding place was between the barn and the kitchen garden, far from all work and fuss. From there, I could see the rounded fields beyond the wall that protected our vegetables; beyond them, you could just make out the curve of other fields stretching all the way to the edge of the forest, which cast its shadow on the purple mountains beyond. By chance, the hollows and humps of the landscape concealed the electric pylons, buildings and roads. Alone in the world, I would spend hours on end reading comics bought in the village shop.

Along with all the staples, the shop displayed objects for which no use had yet been found. Victims of the cruel laws of the market, they slowly gathered dust on the floor-level shelves. I had an enormous respect for Mr Florian and his wife, believing everything in the shop to be their personal property, that they could take whatever they liked from the sweet jars – open a bar of chocolate or screw the cap off a little bottle of Orangina whenever they fancied. Each week, when they handed me my comic book, *Journal de Spirou*, carefully rolled up and bound by a rubber band to make it easier to carry, I felt grateful to them for granting me the pleasure of so precious an item.

The comics invariably finished with "TO BE CONTINUED",

their adventures halted in mid-action. Above the hero – the knight, the young Roman or the cowboy; the reporter, the scout or the paranormal investigator – would be a huge speech bubble containing an "AH!" or an "OH!" or a "DRAT!" They could all see some danger, some extraordinary event, perhaps the solution to their problems, only to be revealed in the next instalment, a week later. Each adventure suspended the course of time, the hero remaining open-mouthed for days, frozen in a state of uncertainty, fear or curiosity.

In the hope that something astounding might happen to me, I had acquired the habit of remaining still for very long periods of time. Motionless on the narrow path that climbed to the forest behind our house, motionless and hidden in the tall grass of the meadow, motionless in the yard in front of the stable – I was waiting. But nothing changed. Our countryside stayed just our countryside. No mysterious stranger, having floated down from the sky in a basket after an immense voyage through space and time, was ever threading his way towards us through the woods. No convertible sports car – complete with cargo of beautiful girls – was ever racing around the corner, pursued by sinister gangsters. No friendly groom ever materialised at the bend in the path, in the company of an exotic animal with extraordinary powers. I might spot a squirrel scampering around a tree trunk, watching me, but, alas, it never exhibited any gift of speech. In the end, I would see my father on his tractor, waving me over to come and help him. Or Sheriff, our dog, dragging his old carcass towards me, wanting to be petted.

That day, I didn't notice Rudy right away, when he came over to show me what he had found on the ground. Rudy spent a lot of time working, and he spent a lot of time doing nothing. During the day, he looked after the animals, refreshing their hay, cleaning the barn, feeding the pigs, repairing the chicken coop and carrying out all the little chores my dad gave him. If he had nothing to do, he observed what was around him with an all-consuming intensity, as though he were straining to impose a little order on the hurried jumble of his thoughts. You could walk in front of him ten times, as he stood there, abnormally static and with his eyes wide open. You could tap him on the shoulder or call out his name, all without him so much as batting an eyelid. Visitors who didn't know Rudy were often seized with panic when they found themselves in the presence of this blank-faced being.

Rudy was the son of a distant cousin in Seeland. He had come to live in our house before I was born. For me he had no age, as if he had never been a child, and would never grow old. His ruddy, thick skin was a barrier that kept him separate from the outside world, and this seemed to me part of a very particular form of beatitude that was his alone.

When I was around eight, I learned that he had Down's Syndrome. By then, I had realised that Rudy's status in our family was different from mine and my sister's. I had already asked our mother why he slept in a bedroom apart from ours, near the pigsty; why he never came anywhere with us except for church on certain Sundays; why he never cried or laughed. She had explained that Rudy possessed, somewhere within his body, an extra something which made him function differently from other people. This careful answer bothered me for years.

Though Rudy had grown into a strong young man, no one in Seeland had wanted to take him on as an apprentice. When my father learned that his cousins were planning to place him in an institution, he decided to bring him back to our farm. Simpletons, idiots, imbeciles and cretins of all kinds made excellent farmhands, he said; it was in their nature to care about animals and vegetables. In hospitals, they just went crazy. But on farms, claimed my father, as the cousins settled the matter over several glasses of plum brandy, they thrived as labourers – had done since the beginning of time.

I was reading a Gil Jourdan detective story when I looked up to see Rudy standing in front of me, busy just watching his hands clasped against his stomach. This was one of his most frequent postures. He would scrutinise his hands for hours, as if these things capable of grasping and manipulating the smallest objects, as well as performing a wide array of other actions, could not be part of his own stiff and stocky person. When he finally noticed that I was looking at him, he showed me the bird he had picked up.

"It's a white pigeon," he said.

I put my book on the ground. "It looks more like a dove. A small dove."

"Dove?"

"Yes. It's a dove."

Rudy had never heard this word. He smiled, happy to have laid hands on something so extraordinary. He was renowned for the tender care he lavished upon our golden leghorn chickens, for whom he was responsible, and for whose comfort he would think up all kinds of fanciful treats. Now, it seemed to disturb him to hold in the hollow of his palms a bird not so different from those in his coop. Incredibly mobile, the bird's tiny head turned 270 degrees. It had immense, protruding eyes, like the two buttons on a stuffed animal. The image of us, projected onto all four corners of its field of vision, no doubt increased the creature's terror. We remained silent for a while. Rudy had immobilised the bird's wings with his thumbs.

"His heart is pounding."

"It's not an animal from around here. It's not a wild bird," I said.

"It's not a wild bird."

These repetitions were a sign of stress, a way for Rudy to lay hold of information and give himself time to think. Usually, though, the repeated words sounded empty in his head, and he understood no more clearly than he had before.

"Sometimes they release white doves for weddings. They put them in a crate, lift the lid, and they fly away all of a sudden."

"... all of a sudden."

"They bring happiness. Or... maybe it's a magician's bird that escaped after his trick went wrong..."

"A magician... yes, a magician," he murmured.

Rudy stared at the dove, as if its proximity to a conjuror might have given it supernatural powers. He opened his hands a little, then quickly raised his arms to throw it into the sky. It should have lifted itself up towards the light, dissolved into the warm mass of air above our heads in a soft whirr of feathers. But, though it unfolded its wings and beat them in the normal way, it gained no height, falling like a stone into the yellow grass.

"Don't do that, Rudy! You'll hurt it!"

As I gathered it up and brushed it off, I felt beneath my fingers the workings of a heart that had gone mad, the bird's palpitating flesh wholly taken over by that one organ and its endless pumping of blood. How terrifying it must have been suddenly to find that it could no longer fly! I noticed its bare rump, sagging a bit obscenely, pink with lots of tiny holes. How could its minuscule brain understand that, without tail feathers, it would never manage more than a pitiful hop?

"No wonder! Look, Rudy," I said, showing him the dove from behind. "It must have been caught by a cat!"

Rudy's eyebrows met in the middle of his forehead in a grimace of concentration. "A cat!" he repeated anxiously, as he made a fruitless inventory of the felines of his acquaintance to try to determine the guilty party.

In my hands, the bird had slowly calmed down. This was a tame dove. It stood up on my palm, and by giving a small, downward jerk, I got it to move onto the other. I repeated the trick several times. It was a skilful creature. No doubt it had often had to find its way through a tube from a tiny cage secreted in a big top hat, to emerge at just the right moment, wreathed in applause, onto a magician's finger. I let it climb onto my shoulder, a rather dominating position that it seemed to enjoy.

"I'm going to keep it."

Rudy reacted by pursing and pouting his always slightly-too-wet lips. Roughly translated, this familiar gesture meant: "Okay. Everything's been said. Let's move on to something else." He turned on his heels and headed purposefully toward the barn, the upper half of his body angled sharply forward. As far as he was concerned, the matter of the bird was over and done with. His attention had been drawn elsewhere, by the noisy arrival in the yard of a woman, carrying a big suitcase.

Under the big elm tree, Sheriff suddenly lifted his tail and ran up barking, as he did when any living being crossed a precise perimeter known only to him. Our dog was named Sheriff because his role was to defend the farm against intruders, a role he played to perfection when we were there to observe him. When none of us was around to admire his expertise, he made no effort at all, and anyone could come and go unmolested. To make Sheriff's status official, we had attached to his collar a marshal's star, with each of its five rays ending in a little round ball. He was an Appenzell sheepdog, in whose coat white was progressively gaining on the black and the brown. He seemed destined to end his old dog's existence with a colourless, monochrome pelt.

Evidently the woman was not familiar with the welcome traditionally extended to strangers arriving at farms. She stood frozen, arms at her side. As soon as Rudy approached, Sheriff ceased his racket and begged for his reward – a rough pat on his head – before returning to his corner of shade, freed from further obligations.

"He... hello! I wanted to speak to the lady of the house. I am..."

From my discreet observation post, I could see that the young woman had just realised she was dealing with a simple-minded person. Rudy was looking straight into her eyes with discomforting intensity, his lower lip overflowing with saliva. She smiled, then continued more quietly and slowly, breaking each word into distinct syllables, as if helping a small child with its spelling.

"My name is Su–zy. Is the la–dy of the house in? I want to speak to her."

Without taking his eyes off her, Rudy removed his cap, carefully smoothed his hair, wet with sweat, to one side, and bowed.

"I..." stammered the woman, increasingly ill-at-ease.

"My name is Rudy."

"Good. Good. Mine is Su–zy."

"Hello, Suzy."

"Hel–lo, Ru–dy."

The introductions were over. The young woman glanced to the right and left in the hope of finding a sensible soul nearby, but she didn't see me. She smiled, but otherwise didn't dare to move. For Rudy, her immobility was merely part of the charm she was weaving over him, which only a magic spell could now break.

Every woman Rudy met, whether young or old, beautiful or ugly, was *the one* who had been long destined for him, yet tragically withheld until just that moment. He often spoke of his future marriage, his eyes wet with happiness. We would tell him reassuringly that he must be patient, but that it would happen, that one day there would be a Mrs Rudy. Meanwhile, he paid court to all the women of the village. They would greet him very politely, never failing to enquire solicitously about his health or his work. These encounters served to convince Rudy of his chances with the opposite sex.

He held out his arm and grasped the free hand of the woman, who was stunned by this sudden gesture of familiarity.

"My name is Rudy."

"That's... that's good! O–kay, Ru–dy. I am go–ing to leave now."

He moved towards her, in search of closer physical contact. The young woman recoiled. If Rudy's hand had not been very firmly gripping her own, she would undoubtedly have fled at top speed.

"Rudy! Leave her alone!" shouted my mother from the door-way. She turned to the woman. "I'm so sorry. He doesn't mean any harm. He's a good boy." Then, addressing Rudy again, she commanded: "Be good! Let the lady go!"

He did so, without taking his eyes off his conquest.

"He can't help touching people for no reason. It's just the way he is," said my mother.

"Yes... Of course."

"I'm so sorry."

"I'm traveling from village to village. I sell plastic containers that can be hermetically sealed. To preserve food. All sizes. They're new. They come from America. Do you...?"

"Why don't you come inside? We'll be more comfortable there. It's cooler."

"Thank you."

"Go right in."

Mum whispered something into Rudy's ear, who obediently replaced his hat on his head. He watched the pair move away with a knowing air. I knew that Mum would have told him, for the hundredth time, that he had to be patient, that someday he would find his soulmate, and that if he wanted it to happen, he had to remain a gentleman and keep a respectful distance from women.

* * *

That night, I went outside to escape the stifling heat in my bedroom. I took my dove, which I had set up on a makeshift perch, an old parrot stand rescued from the back of a shed. The bird had quickly adapted to it, taking turns to perch on each of its six brackets. Its brain held no more than the minimum quantity of necessary information, so that it functioned efficiently, like all of nature's simple mechanisms.

The heat that had accumulated during the day now rose freely up to the sky. A warm wind, sequinned with burning particles, swooped down from the mountains, like the breath of a huge animal crouching in the shadows. The distant stars offered no comfort. They looked like tiny fires.

A window shutter on the ground floor banged. The dove immediately carried out a quick inspection of itself on my shoulder, stretching its head in every direction. The dance appeared to be part of a mating display. I clapped my hands, and it automatically repeated the sequence, with gusto, as if spurred on by hundreds of invisible encouragements. I clapped again, then again and again. Each time, the dove performed several rotations of its head, with an accompanying sound of tiny gears being shifted.

No doubt it had no special attachment to me personally. Perhaps it even took me for its former master, the magician, now magically transformed into a thirteen-year-old boy. Still, I was pleased to discover that it had been trained to do these circus movements.

"Is anyone out there?"

It was Mum's voice. I stepped back to hide in the shadow of the eaves. She leaned out of the window and gave the yard a quick survey. From my position, I could make out a part of the inside of my parents' bedroom. Mum was getting ready to go to bed; Dad must have been asleep already.

Its head nestled in the hollow of its shoulders, heavy eyelids descending at regular intervals, my dove was calm again. Its white plumage reflected the moonlight with unearthly clarity.

Now, Mum was standing in front of her mirror. Arms raised, she slowly undid her hair, fluffing it up in expansive gestures to revive it. Leaning to one side, she brushed it carefully, then stayed still for a while. Framed by the window, she stood exactly beneath the lamp, whose yellow-orange glow lit the nape of her neck, her bare shoulders and her dark armpits. It was as though she were communing with her nocturnal aspect, so different from the one imposed by her mundane, daytime tasks. It had been years since I'd seen her even a little undressed. Even when I was sick and she had to give me medicine in the middle of the night, she would put on one of the dresses she wore during the day.

Mum disappeared. The light remained lit for a long time before it was extinguished. I swallowed. More and more overcome by sleep, my dove was visibly shrinking.

The dark, empty window was like an orphan on the house's façade. I couldn't take my eyes off it, as I imagined, incomprehensibly jealous, my mother beneath the sheets, next to the powerful, heavy body of my father.

II

There were two mornings at home. The first belonged to the cats and to Dad. Always the earliest out of bed, he'd go downstairs and get to work. He would find Rudy in the barn, the pigsty or the shed. The floorboards in the house would creak a little, a door would scrape, and in the winter there would be the weak light of lanterns from the outbuildings.

Some time later, Mum would get up to prepare the first meal, initiating a second phase of general awakening. I would go and join her in the kitchen. Then Dad would come back in, flanked by Rudy, who would immediately take his seat at the end of the table, a little apart from the rest of us. With them, a gust from the outside entered the room, the smell of straw and animals mixing with the steam from the coffee. In my memory, this aroma was something powerful, that instilled goodwill in all of us. My sister, Léa, was always last to arrive, because she went to school on a moped, because she often slept late and didn't eat in the mornings, and because she could always find good reasons not to take part in our shared life.

Breakfast was always the same. Large enough to banish our early-morning fatigue and set us up for the day, it consisted of *rösti* and very milky coffee. Rudy would cut his share into slices, before soaking them and gulping them down, with his head just a few centimetres above his bowl. This dish was a relic of our Bernese origins, imported by the ancestor who, having been chased from his own lands on the other side of the Sarine river, had bought the farm at the beginning of the last century. Ever since this founding act, three generations of us had grown up speaking French with the local accent, yet without adopting the local breakfast of buttered bread and jam.

As I came into the kitchen, Mum would look quickly over her shoulder from her position at the stove. She knew from my footsteps that it was me, but it made me happy to receive this little glance that allowed me to say "Hello, Mum," and her to reply without having to interrupt her work.

That morning, Mum put down the frying pan in which the potatoes were browning, wiped her hands carefully with a kitchen towel, and walked over to where I was sitting.

"Is it a dove?"

"Yes."

She stretched out an arm to stroke its belly. "Where did you find it?"

"Rudy found it."

"Have you given it a name?" she asked, brushing her fingers along the bird's smooth, round back.

The dove began to coo, a faint but deep sound that made its feathers vibrate.

"You should give it a name."

"Um... I don't know."

"It looks wounded."

"Yeah. A cat."

"Are you planning to keep it?"

"Yes."

Mum took out a tiny square of crumpled cloth from her apron pocket. She blew into it carefully and delicately, as if it were an avant-garde musical instrument and she hoped to bring forth a beautiful melody. Her nose was always slightly pink, irritated by the constant friction of handkerchiefs, and its own internal secretions. In the dusty summer heat, her breathing was wheezy and encumbered, as though the air were reluctant to pass in and out of her. In any case, there wasn't a lot of room in her frail chest, which seemed too small to contain lungs. She went back to attend to her pans, sizzling on the hob.

Incredibly tiny in her light-blue dress dotted with pale flowers, my mother wandered adrift in a world of giants. Everything around her – the stove, the stone sink with its complicated taps, the stoneware pots lined up on the shelf, the beams in the ceiling, the big wooden table at which I sat – was on a different scale. When she bent forward, a rosary of vertebrae would appear on her straining neck, just below her black hair wrapped carefully in a bun. That I had lived inside her womb for many months, that I could have emerged from such a slender being, seemed nothing less than a miracle. Mum looked like a little girl.

I was glad that she had petted my dove, accepted its presence without argument. Mum was always busy with a multitude of tasks that no doubt helped to keep her from feelings of despair. I would have liked to be in the bird's place. I would have liked her to set down her towel and dry her hands, to come over and kiss me, stroke my hair, tickle my neck with the tips of her fingers. When I left for school, she would give me a dry peck on the cheek, a kiss from the very tip of her lips that echoed in the cool morning. Lingering on my skin for less than a millisecond, her mouth imparted no sense of its moistness. She never gave me a tender pat of encouragement to send me on my way. Handing me my lunch-box, she would wish me a good day. As I walked past our big elm tree in the garden, I knew without needing to check that she was not watching me go, but had already returned to her chores.

We knew, because she had told us, that Mum dreamed of an easier, less narrow life for my sister and me. Although I felt sure she loved me, I had to go back to when I was very little to remember her arms around me – the times when she would take me down from a hay-ride and hold me up in the air, pressing me against her for an instant before putting me down.

Then, without wanting to, I grew up. The moment I began to look vaguely like a man, all physical contact between us stopped. This did not happen gradually, but from one day to the next, though I have forgotten precisely what prompted the transition.

Dad came in, followed by Rudy, bringing with them the odour of the stable to mingle with the indoor smells. They sat down in silence.

"Where did you find that bird?" asked Dad.

"Rudy gave it to me. I don't know – near the barn..."

Dad lifted his head and glanced at Rudy, who didn't react. He was wholly absorbed by the meticulous ingestion of his food, which required him to take control of each morsel with his mind in order to guide it successfully into his stomach.

"It's a dove."

"Yeah."

"It doesn't have any tail feathers."

"Yeah." I fixed my attention on the back of my mother, who was washing dishes in the sink.

"It was lucky."

"Yeah."

"If the bone had been damaged..."

"The bone?"

"Yes, the bone. If a bird breaks a bone, it's a goner – it slowly dies of asphyxia... Their skeletons are full of air to help them fly. One tear and they empty out." Dad's face disappeared behind his raised bowl.

"Of air?"

"That's right. They have air-filled skeletons. So... you're planning to keep it there on your shoulder, are you, like Robinson Crusoe's parrot?"

"Yeah."

"Its leg muscles look all right. The feathers will grow back. It'll fly again."

"Really?"

"What are you planning to do with it?" he asked, soaking a forkful of *rösti* in his coffee.

"With the dove?"

"Yes, with the dove! You're not really going to lug it around on your shoulder all day, are you?"

"I found a perch for it... a hat-stand from the guest-room."

"Hmm!" Dad gulped down the rest of his dunked *rösti*, tilting back his head, then looked at me. With the back of his hand, he wiped away the brownish stream of coffee that snaked down his chin, and that, on countless occasions, I had watched dribble down his neck, before falling onto his chest and disappearing into the wide-open collar of his checked shirt. I knew he was thinking about the holidays that had just started. The holidays that the authorities, in their immense wisdom, had conceived so that sons could help their fathers in the fields throughout the busy summer months. As far as he was concerned, I was at his service.

"You can take Bagatelle for a walk this morning."

"Okay."

"She hasn't been out for two days."

"Sure. I'll get her moving again."

"Then you can come and help me with the chicks."

"Okay."

"They're suffering in the heat. We'll have to remove the dead ones..."

Dad's dream was to live with his family on an isolated farm amidst meadows and fields surrounded by dense forests. He was fond of saying that civilisation was born with agriculture. When nomadic groups stopped chasing after herds of game and settled in one place, they had started to treat nature as something that belonged to them. All humanity's progress, he would say, had been made possible thanks to the perseverance of the early farmers. Historians had always undervalued these stubborn labourers, who moulded the landscape and nourished others so that they could devote themselves to more visible and prestigious jobs. It was these men of the land who had fed Charlemagne and Napoleon, and countless other kings and emperors. Without a good square meal on their plates, they would never have had the strength to rule over their vast empires. As for their castles and cathedrals, they too were built by workers who relied on farm produce to give them energy for their exhausting tasks.

The early farms, he would say, had been like little universes exempt from external influence, self-sufficient places where all the necessities of existence could be had. It was farmers who cultivated the idea of liberty – liberty being just another word for independence. Was it any wonder that these same proud breeders and farmers had one day risen up from their pastures in central Switzerland, to slough off tyranny and plant the seeds of a democracy that would change the face of the world?

Dad was convinced that roast chicken, at that time rarely served except at the ceremonial Sunday dinner tables of the bourgeoisie, could not long escape the forces of democratisation. With people earning more and more, meat consumption would naturally increase, and poultry would become a daily habit for the expanding middle classes. On the back of this logic, he had borrowed several hundred thousand francs to invest in a new hen-house. He would buy ten thousand downy chicks at a time, all female, fatten them up, and sell them five months later to a buyer who would kill them, skin them and chop them up, ready to grace the shelves of the supermarkets. We all knew that our future depended on the efficient force-feeding of this vast multitude of fowl.

"Then what?'

"What?"

"Then what are you going to do with yourself?"

"I don't know. Maybe some drawing."

Dad pushed his plate and bowl into the middle of the table and stood up, muttering to himself. He seemed to expand a little when he was annoyed, like a cat with its fur sticking up, as if his large, muscular body physically absorbed his anger. Before the events of that summer of 1976, I had never seen him get cross. Maybe he had never learned, or it just wasn't in his nature. He would merely blink a little as he took whatever blow fortune had dealt, then cast a mocking look over the world with his light-blue eyes, before resuming one of the hundred chores that always needed to be done on the farm. He called that "taking charge".

As he was leaving the room, Dad made a detour to touch Mum lightly and kiss her quickly on the back of her neck. We heard the door slam at the end of the hallway, then the muffled yaps of Sheriff, who was always transported with joy at the sight of someone putting on his boots.

Bagatelle lived alone in a stable at the top of the village, opposite what we called the castle. This was actually a tall, pot-bellied house with massive walls that had protected the lords of the region in the Middle Ages. The owners, from the minor nobility, must have felt somewhat insecure, since they'd thought it advisable to fortify not only the house, but its adjoining barn, too. My grandfather, Annibal – called Anni by everyone in the village – lived in a tiny upstairs flat in its old hayloft. A cousin barely younger than he was, Rose, came to do his cleaning and cooking. I glanced up before I entered the stable, but his shutters were closed.

"Hey, Bagatelle! It's me!" I announced.

My greeting wasn't enough to shake the mare out of her apathy. Was she lonely? Or had years of inactivity brought about a profound and absolute emotional indifference? I stood next to her head to give her a chance to recognise me. My deformed reflection, as if from the curve of a spoon, gazed at me from her big black eyes, from which a thick yellow liquid streamed constantly, hardening at the edges and sticking to eyelids she could no longer close. Bagatelle was very short-sighted, having spent much of her working life in blinkers.

I stroked her white muzzle for a while, and something began to awaken in her immense, stiff body. Muscles quivered under her skin. Her breathing grew a little stronger.

"Yes, yes! We're going out!"

She would soon be twenty-seven. My grandfather, unable to imagine a farm without a horse, had bought her in the early 1950s just as the rest of the village was equipping itself with up-to-date tractors and it was becoming easy to rent machinery. In his day, he had always worked with Bagatelle to break up the earth with the harrow, or to turn over the hay where the land sloped steeply. Now the big, four-pronged pitchforks leaned against a wall in the stable, gathering dust.

Unable either to close her eyes or lie down to sleep because she wouldn't be able stand up again, Bagatelle seemed to be awaiting her own death. She stood stiff and straight, as if cast in bronze, alive yet strangely frozen. I wondered if her head were full of nostalgic images of flowering meadows and wild stampedes. Bagatelle's static existence seemed to have abnormally stimulated her sweat glands; she gave off a powerful odour that permeated everything. Each strand of straw in her litter, each stone in the wall, each board in the stable – they all smelled strongly of horse. Depending on the direction of the wind, these acrid emanations were noticeable even on the road several dozen metres away. Not at all put out, my dove remained calmly perched on my shoulder; birds, I reasoned, probably didn't perceive smells as we did. Or maybe this particular specimen, during its long career as a magician's assistant, had worked in a circus amidst a ring of horses? Or with other wild animals whose smells were even more pungent and alarming?

My eyes hadn't yet adapted to the darkness. As I groped mechanically for the halter on its hook, I stepped on something unfamiliar in the straw, something solid that immediately shrank back. For a fraction of a second, I imagined that some wild animal, a lion or a panther, was hiding in the litter, about to pounce on me. But only for a fraction of a second, because then my grandfather slowly emerged, covered in straw and dust, like a stick of caramel rolled in sugar.

"That's not nice! You shouldn't step on people like that!"

"I... How was I supposed to know you were there?"

"Ow! You hurt me, you know! Not very nice at all!"

"I'm telling you I didn't see you. Anyway, why were you hiding under the straw?"

My grandfather looked me up and down. His pale, grey eyes were surmounted by thick, bushy eyebrows that were always mobile, and expressed the whole gamut of his emotions. Ever since he had handed over the farm to Dad, it had been a point of honour for him not to get involved, to leave his son in absolute control. When he stopped by our house, he never said anything about the running of the business, as if it had never belonged to him. He would walk up the yard with long strides, sometimes follow Dad into the pigsty or the barn, but he would never pick up a tool or carry a milk can or give any advice. Not that Dad asked him for any. Looking back, it seems to me that Anni, the only grandson of the ancestor who had migrated from the German part of Switzerland, was rejecting his own past as a farmer, that he didn't want to think about how he'd spent his entire life. Almost all of his utterances were in the negative.

He ran his fingers through his short white hair, which made him look like an old American senator, and extricated a handful of straw and manure. Over the years he had lost every ounce of spare flesh. He could have been made of wood, or some other fibrous material, so completely had his skeleton taken over his person. At the same time, he gave an impression of toughness and durability: not many diseases could take root in a being thus stripped of all its soft parts.

"It's too hot upstairs."

"So you slept here?"

"It's much nicer – moist and quite cool. It isn't doing anyone any harm."

"Of course not."

"You're not going to take her out, are you?"

"I'm taking her for a little walk. Like every morning."

"Ah yes. We wouldn't want her to forget how to wiggle her bum, would we?" He noticed my bird. "You're not taking that dove, are you?"

"I am."

He took hold of it firmly by the wings, turned it over as if looking for a label with some product information, then returned it to my shoulder. It gave no reaction. Maybe it was scared stiff at the prospect of being crushed by hands as horny as a raptor's claws? Still, I would have preferred it to be less docile. It was a little too happy to be approached by strangers.

"Okay, I'm going now. Do you need anything?"

"No. Rose will be here soon. I'd better not forget to go back up to my rooms."

I attached the halter to Bagatelle's harness, stroking her neck all the while. She didn't budge. I pulled. Nothing. I pulled again.

Anni pressed up against her ear, smoothing her muzzle, and whispered: "*Kopf hoch! Graduus u gueti Reis!*"[1]

Bagatelle's neck tensed. The rest of her arthritis-crippled body followed suit, as she came back to life, bit by bit, until walking became possible. The moment she took her first step, she urinated and defecated copiously.

This was supposedly one of the benefits of our walks. As we went along, Bagatelle would periodically empty herself, like some kind of manure-making machine. My father insisted that I gather up this precious material with a little shovel and bag, since it was the ideal fertilizer for our vegetable garden. I found it humiliating to bend down behind the withered rump of our old mare, and tried to get out of this chore whenever I could.

It was only half past seven, but the morning was already

---

1 Head up! Off you go and *bon voyage*!

23

hot. We were roasting under the arid sky. A thick mist of sweat hovered over Bagatelle's back. I walked along beside her, seeing only the landscape to my left, half of my field of view obstructed by her voluminous paunch. Without any moisture to carry them through the atmosphere, noises no longer sounded the same. The horseshoes made only tiny clicking sounds as they struck the asphalt. Our world was being reduced to the essential, was becoming a mere sketch of reality. The roads and paths on which a tiny, colourful dot sometimes passed by; the dark line of the river, its steep banks overhung by black, motionless trees; the fields of wheat and the yellow-streaked pastures, their borders neatly marked by thickets and hedges. Everything was as clear as pen-strokes on a white page. The sun had wrung the landscape dry, worn nature down to the bone.

Bagatelle stopped on the patch of grass at the edge of the village, near the fountain in the shade of the big lime tree. For the old mare, this wasn't just some grass under a tree: it was a magic square, the goal of all her walks, a horizon beyond which she could not pass, the place her steps always led her. There wasn't a single flower, as if they had all decided to stay underground until next year. Not a breath of air passed through the branches, motionless and silent above us. I sat down on a rock. My dove began to beat its wings frantically, so I moved it onto Bagatelle. It made a few dance steps on her rump before settling calmly into the hollow of her back, looking as proud as an ox-pecker on a rhinoceros. I went back to my rock and took out my sketchpad and pencil.

A little orange Renault 5 passed by on the road. I watched it drive alongside the trees. When it began the curve to descend towards the fields, it stopped, as if my gaze had cut its power. I distinctly heard the grinding of the gears, then a high-pitched squeal as it reversed to draw level with me. A woman in her early thirties emerged. She closed the door gently, as if to avoid waking someone inside, then glanced at Bagatelle, before heading towards me.

"Is that your horse?"

"Well, it's Bagatelle..."

"Bagatelle! What a great name. Is he a bit of a womaniser then?"[1]

"Oh... no... she's a very old mare... I'm just..."

"Are you Gus?"

"You... You know who I am?"

"Of course I know. You are Auguste Sutter. Also known as Gus..."

"... by people close to me."

She bent down in front of me, her chest a few centimetres from my knees. She smiled.

"My name is Cécile."

Suddenly I felt overwhelmed by the dense mystery of her eyes. Stripped of all personality, I might as well have been an animal – a kitten you could give a name to and stroke right away, without having to get to know it first. Her face was very close to mine. I breathed in her perfume. It was a sweet, flowery perfume; the smell of dew-covered meadows waking up under the morning sun. Because of the drought, our minds were full of dreams of coolness and moisture: of lush prairies, cascading waterfalls and ploughed fields transformed into rice paddies by rain. Rudy would sometimes stand motionless while he stared at the horizon, blinking his eyes in his own special way, his features hollowed out. When you asked him what he was staring at, he'd reply, in all seriousness, that just over there, between the fields, was a big lake he had never seen before.

Cécile wore a full-cotton patchwork dress that came down to her ankles, with a brightly-coloured plaid pattern in cranberry

---

1 The primary meaning of *bagatelle* is "trinket", but it is also an informal term for sex.

and tobacco brown. It narrowed at the neck, which only served to thrust her chest further forwards. A belt made of large pearls, the golden colour of amber, floated loosely around her hips. Her tanned breasts, close together and shining with sweat, were a living echo of the dead stones that adorned her waist.

"It's nice here under the leaves in this heat, isn't it? Look how still they are – as if they're trying not to move so they can give us better shade... So... You know, I'm a friend of your mother's."

"Oh!"

"You have a handsome little face. She wasn't lying... It's incredible, the silence here. Maybe it's because there isn't a breath of wind. Anyway, it's quite pleasant. We could stay here not talking and there would be nothing in our ears. As if the air were dead. Don't you think? What are you drawing? Can I see?"

"Well..."

"Go on! I'm not going to eat you."

I showed her my drawing.

I had reduced Bagatelle to a bare minimum of swift lines, while adding three of four vertebrae to her neck. I had faithfully rendered her powerful hindquarters, but made her head and mane smaller, to transform her into a young Appaloosa with a dappled coat. It was mounted by a young Nez Perce Indian girl, who was looking behind her with one hand resting on its rump. On her wrist was a bird of prey. You could make out some movement in a thicket, but I was the only one who knew that the girl's attention had been caught by the fearsome cougar concealed there.

"Wow, that's amazing! There must be something special about your eyes, inventing things that don't exist. Amazing. I mean it! You're right – it's boring, always having to look at the same things. We should imagine other colours, extra bits and pieces everywhere, so we can keep up our sense of wonder at just being alive. Of course, there are people who swallow things for that... Here, look – why don't you colour in the fountain? And you could decorate the tree and the horse..."

"The horse is an Appaloosa. A prairie horse..."

"You're a wizard. I mean it. You really know what you're doing. Indian stories are my favourite."

The woman turned her attention to Bagatelle. "Hey, look – there's a bird on your horse! It's a turtledove. Is it yours too?"

"Yes! It's a dove. It's trained," I replied quickly, before her mind leaped on to something else.

"Can you show her to me? I love birds. You know they're directly descended from dinosaurs. If you watch them carefully, you'll see they still have something dinosaur-like about them. The feet, the long neck, the mobile head, and so on. They come from primeval times. They survived because they learned how to fly. That's a great lesson, don't you think? Now might be a good time for people to start learning it too. Imagine! Birds are the only animals that sing. They really sing, complete melodies. That's because they know how to fly. They still haven't got over being able to go up in the sky, so they can't stop singing!"

Cécile clasped my dove in her hands as if to press it and extract its juice, then lifted to her lips and kissed it on its beak. Unfazed, the bird gently pecked her mouth, stretching out its neck.

"Oh, poor thing! It's all shaved at the back! You didn't tear out its feathers to stop it flying away, did you?"

"No. I found it like that. It's wounded... It was probably a cat."

She turned it over and caressed its pink, naked flesh, as repulsive as the fatty, thick, slightly sticky skin of a plucked chicken. All of a sudden, the dove tensed up, as if being touched on this denuded part of its anatomy had triggered its flight reflex by reminding it of its predator.

"Calm down, my pretty little thing!"

We were interrupted by Bagatelle who, monumental under the sun, emptied herself noisily and without the slightest quiver. A multitude of smoking little balls dropped one on top of the other to form a perfect cone behind her.

"Well! What a joyful process! I love the smell of manure, don't you? It's very strange because it doesn't smell bad, just of horse. It makes me think of the Knie circus where I used to go with my parents when I was little. A horse eats nothing but grass. That's why the manure smells good. It's the smell of the fields. Not like all those animals that eat meat, that eat corpses, in other words putrefying matter, corruption... Well, there's another side to life too... I have to go."

She set my dove carefully on Bagatelle's rump, and ran her hand through my hair as if to ruffle it. Looking straight into my eyes, she gave me a big, loud, slow kiss on each cheek. I inhaled her breath. It smelled of honey and liquorice.

* * *

I spent the first part of the afternoon helping Dad with Rudy at the hen-house. It was on the edge of the forest, in the only field that actually belonged to us. For most of the day it remained in shadow, and my grandfather had only been able to buy it because no one else in the village had wanted it.

Before installing the first brood, Dad had invited Anni to come and admire the long, flat building with its wide triangular roof, like a house buried in the ground with only its uppermost three metres protruding. Anni had arrived on foot, having walked from his place because he refused to travel in any other way. He had toured the site in silence next to Dad, while he very proudly explained the system of aeration and automatic feeding, and pointed out the grain as it flowed through various aluminium tubes into suspended dishes, with a noise like Indian maracas. I remember seeing how Dad, at least twice Anni's size, waited for a word of congratulation or encouragement, kicking little pebbles with the tip of his shoe against the metal wall. But my grandfather only lit a cigarette, then sighed noisily amidst a cloud of smoke, without uttering a single comment.

Our gigantic incubator had no windows. Once inside, we felt like adventurers exploring a mysterious planet far from our own solar system, a planet whose atmosphere might be made up of harmful gases or mutant bacteria with the power to penetrate our tissues and take over our bodies. And perhaps we really weren't quite ourselves in this extra-terrestrial environment, due to the strict hygienic measures needed to keep out the germs that, if introduced to the main nesting or feeding areas, could transform a healthy chicken into an unsellable, raddled carcass in a single day.

First, we would enter a disinfection chamber, a narrow room with tiled walls, where we would get undressed and shower. We would always have to call Rudy several times to get him to leave the stream of hot water beneath which, abandoned to pleasure, he would forget everything, above all the reason he was taking a shower. Then we'd put on special boots, white overalls, gloves, and a ridiculous cotton hat to cover all our hair, before going to work among the thick cloud of hens shuffling in all directions over the concrete floor, around the lines of pipes and the dishes hanging from the ceiling by long metal wires reaching almost to the ground. Large ventilators fanned the air to keep the temperature constantly between 20 and 25 degrees.

On that day, we extracted a dozen or so dead hens, some of them pecked to death by fellow hens seized by a cannibalistic urge. After collecting them in a huge bag, Dad loaded them onto the little trailer behind our Toyota. He wasn't happy. It was getting too hot in the vast hen-house, dulling the appetite of the birds, which weren't fattening up quickly as he'd hoped. The buyer from the supermarket negotiated the price according to the quality of the merchandise, and he might refuse to pay for scrawny chickens or for birds whose flesh was too dense and tough.

On the way back, Dad glanced behind several times to check that our load was stable. Whenever he took off his white jump-suit, I thought a part of his soul remained captive in the little pile crumpled at his feet.

We drove over a pothole that shook the car. The tow-bar made a loud cracking noise and our trailer flew into the air. The bag flew open, and the dead hens were ejected. As he stepped on the brakes, Dad watched in the rear-view mirror these piti-ful attempts at posthumous flight, ending with heavy falls into the grass on the side of the road. I felt a pang in my heart at the thought of my dove with its useless wings. The corpses were scat-tered in grotesque positions. Rudy picked up the empty bag. Dad stood with his arms at his sides. I saw his eyes were full of water, like two big sponges, and quickly looked away. Rudy didn't know what to do either, and for a while the three of us stood, silent, upright and motionless in the middle of this open-air cemetery.

The border between the human and the animal world was thin and fragile, Dad would frequently tell us, and because of that we had to respect it. Sometimes, on summer nights when the daylight kept us working late, or on winter nights when our heated, well-lit farm seemed despite its solid foundations to sway a little in the wind, Dad would wax lyrical about the Celts and the Illyrians, the first occupants of these still-virgin lands. They had worshipped as a god each hill, glade, forest, mountain, waterfall, lake, tree and plain; but they had viewed the animals as independent peoples, with whom they had to make pacts. One day my sister, when she was little, had talked about a cow "giving birth". Dad had taken her shoulders firmly in his hands and, staring straight into her eyes, made her repeat several times, like a lesson that had to be learned by heart: "A cow calves. When a cow has a calf, it *calves*!"

The dead hens in the dry grass looked as though they had never been animals. The stunted, twisted, pale bodies were no longer part of nature; they were no different from the assorted colourful rubbish at the municipal dump. The ancient pact had been broken.

Maybe it was pity – or else the sun beating down on our heads – that finally shook us out of our inertia. Rudy, trotting along behind us with tiny, mincing steps, held the bag open as we gathered up the corpses for a seond time. Back in the car, Dad said nothing, but as he wiped away with a forearm the drops of sweat from his shining forehead, it seemed to me that they were a substitute for tears.

III

Rudy was showing me a gaping crack he had found in the ground. We were in front of the barn, where the earth, pounded by the daily comings and goings of the cows, was smooth as stone.

"Look, you can put all your fingers inside!" Rudy stared at me urgently, his hand buried in the fissure. "Try!"

I bent down opposite him, and inserted my hand up to the knuckles. "It's deep, isn't it?"

"Yes! Very."

"And warm."

"Yes. Even at the bottom it's warm."

Rudy's features had arranged themselves in a way I had never seen before. They conveyed a mixture of incredulity and anxiety. The complexity of the situation far exceeded his comprehension, so that his face could express only an elementary, naked fear that made me think of the very first men on earth. It was the fear of Rahan, hero of my comic books, who strove to survive in an age when nothing that happened could be explained, among erupting volcanoes, shaggy, sabre-toothed monsters, and giant birds capable of lifting into an electric sky prey as large as buffalo. Rudy was closely related to this very ancient humanity. There was no doubt that he imagined that this first, small cleft could at any moment start to spread rapidly, branching out like the cracks made by an impact on glass. The whole known world – for him, the village and the fields around the village – might be torn asunder beneath our very feet, to be hurled into the planet's flaming core. I knew that he had the imagination to generate such thoughts.

"Look, Rudy," I said, tapping the ground with my foot. "The earth is hard as a turtle's shell. That's why it's cracking."

This image of a living creature opening up like an overripe fruit made Rudy's mouth gape in horror. I had used a bad example.

"It's like a stone! A stone can't change shape. When it freezes, it just cracks open…"

This didn't put his mind at rest either. If mere cold could make a rock as brittle as a wafer, there was definitely nothing certain beneath our feet. Rudy stared at me.

"Look, the earth is bare here. But in the fields, there's grass, trees… It's the plants that hold the ground in place… There's no danger," I added finally.

Rudy looked around at the threadbare fields and bushes, shrivelled as if after a fire. My explanations were not helping. How could this dying vegetation, with its feeble roots, possibly stop the ground from tearing apart?

It turned out that the best way to rescue Rudy from this mental maelstrom was to distract him. The buzz of Léa's moped as it climbed the road, then its noisy, sputtering arrival in the yard, instantly dissipated his geological anxieties.

Sheriff rushed furiously over to meet my sister, who was returning from a musical rehearsal. Her teacher had persuaded her to play as second violin in a collaborative performance between our own musicians and an orchestra from the German Democratic Republic. It was an honour, and a heavy responsibility. Léa was living only for this moment. It was the big event of her summer of 1976 – to play before an exclusive audience as part of an important cultural exchange which would symbolise the recent normalisation of diplomatic relations between the two states.

Sheriff's tail unrolled, a sign of ardent affection. He leapt into the air, shifting the weight of his body from one paw to the other, to try to get Léa to play with him. Ignoring him, she rode straight past, raising a long snake of dust behind her. Hopping and barking madly, Sheriff followed for a few metres. All of a sudden, he lurched and sank to the ground, as soundlessly as a drop of oil.

"Oh!" said Rudy.

We stared at the place where the dog had fallen, as if we were at the cinema, and the frozen image would simply start up again after a brief technical hitch. When it became clear that Sheriff wasn't about to get up, we ran over. Rudy knelt down to feel the air all around him, in search of the invisible wall against which he must have just crushed his muzzle. He massaged the dog's body, took his head in his hands, then finally laid him down again to touch all his extremities in turn. Terrified, he turned to me.

"His paws are wet!"

How could Sheriff have wet paws when he hadn't been splashing around in the rain? Rudy began to get upset. He stood up, knelt down, then stood up again, in an effort to allay his anxiety. For him, anything out of the ordinary threatened disaster.

"Calm down! Calm down! It's nothing serious. Look, Rudy, his eyelids are closed!"

Compulsively, Rudy continued to bend down and get up.

"He's still breathing. If he were dead, his eyes would be open. His eyes are closed. He's sleeping. Rudy. Sheriff is sleeping!"

I caught hold of his hand, and made him kneel down to place it on our dog's stomach.

"Look. Eyes closed. He's calm. He's breathing. He's sleeping…"

"…"

"See! I'll say it again. He's sleeping!"

"…"

"If he were dead, his eyes would be open."

"He's sleep… sleep… sleeping," stammered Rudy.

"Yes, yes. That's good, isn't it? He's breathing."

Léa propped up her moped in front of the house, and strolled over to join us, holding her violin.

"What are you doing?"

"Sheriff fainted!"

"Dogs don't faint. He's either alive or he's dead."

Rudy stood up rapidly.

"Shut up, Léa!" I shouted.

She was standing a few feet away, in her close-fitting black dress that left her shoulders bare and showed off her modest chest. She always wore this dress to her music lessons, as if she were already performing in front of an admiring audience. Léa was as thoroughly indifferent to Sheriff as she was to all the other animals on the farm. This had begun soon after she turned eleven, the moment she had felt inside her the first premature stirrings of her femininity. Since then she had not touched a single one of our animals, as if they were suddenly taboo because they were secretly linked to the forces of nature at work within her own body.

Or maybe she was just putting on airs and graces. If a chicken had the impudence to come too close while Léa was reading one of her magazines on the deck-chair in the garden, she would scream at it. No doubt the creature reminded her all too vividly that she wasn't sunning herself in Deauville, but on a patch of grass between the slurry ditch and the barnyard.

It was terrible to see Sheriff sighing after Léa. Somewhere in his faithful-companion brain must have been a memory of the time of her innocence, when she would throw him sticks and he would bring them back in exchange for an armful of cuddles. Now, she either ignored him, or else she actively avoided him. If she shoved him away to stop him jumping onto her legs, he would always linger a few feet off, in the hope of some further encouraging gesture. His persistence filled me with despair. Sometimes he would suffer for hours on end at Léa's feet, emitting occasional soft whines, or sighing like a rejected suitor.

My sister made a clear distinction between culture and nature. Since I spent a lot of my time with Rudy and sometimes fed the pigs or walked Bagatelle, I belonged firmly in the second category. It didn't make a difference that I devoted most of my free time to drawing. Rudy and I were too much part of the material world that she was trying to reject.

"Just wait a moment, you imbeciles!"

Léa took her violin out of its case. Shiny black on the outside, burgundy velvet inside, it always reminded me of a small coffin. She flourished her bow in the air like a magic wand.

"What are you doing?"

"Simple. I'm going to wake him up."

"You're crazy."

"Shut up! You don't have a clue anyway."

"Yeah, right."

She began to play, swaying her upper body rhythmically, as if she were rousing a snake from a basket. During one *allegro con fuoco* passage, she almost started to leap up and down on the spot, attacking the strings with abrupt, staccato blows. Pigeons flew up from behind the barn and headed for the shelter of the woods. Sheriff, wholly insensitive to the music of Dvořák, didn't budge.

Léa stopped playing. She packed away her instrument with exaggerated respect, thus signalling the scorn she felt towards us. I think she sincerely believed that she now had an important role in East-West *rapprochement* and the brotherhood of all peoples.

"It's not my problem – you sort it out!" she said, as she flounced off.

Rudy looked at me in consternation. Then he turned his attention to Sheriff. He felt his nose, which was dripping.

"We should put him in the shade."

Rudy gathered him up with a ease and a gentleness that surprised me, and carried him under the big elm.

"What if we poured cold water on him?"

Rudy ran to the shed and came back with a full watering can.

"Go on, then!" I said.

He couldn't make up his mind to do it.

"Go on, Rudy. Like we do for lettuce..."

Still Rudy hesitated, unable to make the connection between vegetables in the ground and Sheriff lying on its surface.

"Give it to me, then! I'll do it."

I poured a fine, delicate rain onto Sheriff's body, keeping the watering can's large nozzle raised up high. The dog opened one eye, and gazed up for a moment in astonishment at our two worried faces against the background of the sky. Twice, he tried and failed to stand up, like a boxer after being flat-out on the canvas, before he finally rediscovered the muscles he needed to rise and shake himself. He stood there, a little unsteady, before Rudy gathered him up again and carried him off to the barn.

* * *

That night, I took my bird outside, in front of the house. The stars were shining with extra vigour, having moved closer to

38

the earth. They were like a multitude of little campfires above our heads. I could just hear, behind the surface of the calm, motionless, burning night, an infinity of faint, dry cracks, as if the fields beaten all day long by the sun were still slowly frying.

I walked along the wall of the vegetable garden, hoping to stir the air around me into motion. With my dove's claws gripping my shoulder, I began to run, thinking to give my bird the sensation of flight, but I soon became exhausted in the excessively close air. I lay down in the short grass; it felt like a bare mattress.

I would have liked to be inside the frame of a cartoon depicting a night-time scene, in which all the moonlit elements were represented in blue. The hero would pass through this landscape in silence: the dark blue trees, the light blue meadows, the dark blue lamp-posts, the light blue street... Even the depths of the shadows would be blue. But there were no cold colours anywhere near me. In the heart of this false darkness, reds and yellows smouldered on, and those summer nights were in reality only faded versions of our days.

The strains of my sister's violin emerged into the night from the open window of the living room. She was practising the *staccato*, with such force that this vaguely Indian melody sounded like a series of whiplashes. I could see her writhing silhouette under the lamp, and my mother's profile too, as she sat listening for the hundredth time to Léa going through Dvora's obsessive notes. They often had long discussions from which I was excluded, and during which my sister would sometimes stroke Mum's arm. I was confused by this gesture, ordinarily deployed to reassure or to calm its recipient, yet which in this case must have a quite different aim, since neither of the two ever seemed particularly agitated. Mum would always listen to my sister playing her violin with her eyes wide open, as if paralysed by some *idée fixe*, at the mercy of a tempestuous inner life whose intensity and violence dazed her. She would sometimes say that the music Léa played had the same colour as her instrument: mahogany brown with lighter streaks that reminded her of the gleaming skin of a newly-shelled conker.

My dove suddenly grew animated on my stomach. Its eyelids fluttered erratically over its protruding eyeballs – far too large to fit inside such a small head – and it began to march and strut about, as if thousands of people were applauding from the bushes. All of a sudden, I felt overwhelmed by too much reality. Under the protection of the night, a black beetle scuttled along, like a plump musical note that had fallen off its score onto the ground, and was now trying to find its way back. I stretched out my leg and crushed it gently with my foot until it burst, telling myself that our destiny on this planet was merely the result of a giant lottery, presided over by a heartless and whimsical creator.

Once a month, Mum would sit at the kitchen table and do the accounts. She would line up the bills, receipts and the two big government ledgers covered with marbled paper, before opening a voluminous black notebook to fill it with numbers. The light from the lamp would fall on her frail neck, making her look like a studious schoolgirl, and a cold silence like that of an empty church would fill the house.

Meanwhile, Dad would bustle to and fro in an attempt to hide his nerves. As if he had just remembered a little task requiring his presence elsewhere, he would tiptoe out of the room, closing the door behind him with infinite gentleness. A few minutes later, he would return just as discreetly, slipping behind Mum's back to look over her shoulder. At last, she would straighten up and give him a smile that squeezed his heart. Then they would talk for a long time about the two columns of figures, and about our precarious financial situation, always in undertones, as if to speak too crudely or concretely about such matters might bring bad luck.

I belonged to this fragile home, in which each person was struggling in their own small, enclosed space. My back was pressed against the hot earth, my eyes looking up at the sky. I told myself that our dreams were like a train entering a station: first glimpsed from afar in a dazzling, dusty light, the train grows ever more solid as it approaches, then glides slowly in front of us for a long time before we know if it will actually stop, and we'll be able to get on.

* * *

I couldn't sleep. I padded across our vast kitchen in my underwear, with the vague idea of drinking a glass of milk. There was a full jug at the back of the fridge. The cold had thickened the liquid, and a layer of wrinkled skin covered its surface, as if, unobserved inside its plastic and aluminium incubator, the milk was slowly re-assuming an animal form. Dad always filled a bucket for our personal use during the early-morning milking. It was un-homogenised, and each day he presented it to us as having come from the udder of a specific cow. He believed that each beast produced a particular vintage, detectable at the first mouthful. He liked to tell us that cows, like humans, are gourmets and have their own food preferences – one never grazing on purple clover, another mad about meadow grass, a third with a taste for cat's-tail.

The fridge hummed in the empty room, from time to time emitting a few chugs followed by a brief, electric shudder of exaltation. Then it would snort like a weary old animal, before settling again into its regular pattern of respiration, each time a little more laboured. The large family dining table, gleaming

41

in the moonlight, was bathed in a strange, somewhat unnerving silence. It looked like an altar awaiting ritual sacrifices.

I opened the fridge door. The coolness of a miniature Arctic paradise, with its blocks of ice, its powdery snow and its steel-grey sky, enveloped me. In an effort to keep its temperature constant, the machine started up again, giving a friendly snort. I moved closer and rested my chest against the freezing metal edge. Exerting more pressure, I let the cold penetrate me and spread through me from my stomach to my extremities. I began to rub myself against every part I could reach, until I disappeared almost completely inside. I wanted to shrink, to squeeze between the jug of milk and the eggs, to rest my neck gently on the slab of butter, to be slowly buried beneath artificial snow as my muscles gradually stiffened.

"Gus! Are you making love to the fridge?"

I jumped back. The yellow light of the fridge cast a long beam that crossed the room to meet the almost equally intense light coming from the window. These two brilliant lines drew an immense X, in the far triangle of which I now saw Cécile, shining with unreal illumination. Her gauzy nightdress clung to her body as though it had been glued on.

Unable to control the torrent of my thoughts, enfeebled by a sudden blast of tormenting heat, I didn't even try to hide the bulge in my pyjamas. A strange connection arose in my head between this woman, lit up amidst the surrounding darkness as on a theatre stage, and the animals that loomed unexpectedly through the mist as you rounded the bend of a forest path. But all these were just fleeting apparitions, figments of my imagination... I closed my eyes. When I opened them, Cécile reappeared exactly in the same place. Coming forward, she said quite naturally, as if she had always occupied our kitchen and I were the one who had improperly established my headquarters there, that she had come downstairs for a drink because she was dying of thirst.

She brushed past me. I breathed in the air displaced by her motion: the odour of her body, a mixture of Indian patchouli and night-time sweat. It was the fragrance of bed. She found the pitcher of milk, turned it the right way, and carried it to her lips to quench her thirst. As she tilted her head back, her breasts rose a little beneath the cloth of her nightdress. They seemed both substantial and strangely airy, almost transparent in the feeble light. A stream of liquid flowed down her chin. Before it broke up into droplets and disappeared inside her nightdress, she wiped her mouth with the back of her hand – a rather manly gesture – looking me straight in the eyes. I think she asked me if I wanted some too; I must have refused. She said she was in search of a little coolness in these apocalyptic temperatures. A paralysing stupor had come over my face. When she was done, she walked up to me, patted my cheek as if to bring my features back to life, and said, "Your mum invited me to sleep here. It was too late to drive back last night." She gave me another smile before leaving the room. I watched her as she moved towards the hallway door, trailing an infinitely long shadow behind her. Without turning back, she called out, "Sleep well, sweetie!"

I stood for a while in the kitchen, looking at the cupboard, the imposing table and chairs, the massive bread bin, before returning slowly to my bedroom, like a snail in the midday sun. I was carrying on my back my parents' farm, a shell much too heavy for my small body. When I threw myself on my sweat-soaked bed, my dove stirred. It didn't seem be able to sleep either, and was nodding back and forth as though it hoped to defeat insomnia by means of this rocking motion. Perhaps it was no longer using enough energy to tire itself out during the day.

Or did these anxious little creatures never really rest? The poor thing was always in a state of alarm. Its tiny brain couldn't grasp that it no longer possessed feathers on its tail to help it escape predators, so that it remained forever pointlessly on guard, as if it were still capable of launching itself high into the sky.

I couldn't sleep. I knew that I had a future, because all thirteen-year-old boys who are leaving their childhood behind them must have a future. I was at the age when you're immortal, with a whole life before you. But now this destination, hitherto distant and unreal, was beginning to acquire clearer outlines. I felt like a comic-strip character advancing towards a far-off landscape that becomes with every frame less vague – and less appealing.

I got up and went to stand at the window. Just after four o'clock, I watched Cécile cross our yard quickly, before disappearing around the scorner. A few moments later, the hoarse engine of her Renault 5 coughed angrily. I listened as she took the main road to the village, before veering left onto the road to Possens. The car's stubborn roar traversed the hillside, then faded slowly and was absorbed into the nothingness.

IV

"Mum..."

"Yes."

"Who is Cécile?"

I was sitting at the table. Dad and Rudy were busy, probably in the barn. My sister was still sleeping, and Mum was cooking the *rösti* with her back to me. She didn't answer right away. Wiping her hands on the front of her apron, she lowered the heat under the frying pan, and turned to face me.

"Cécile..." she whispered, then fell silent.

She was wearing a little blue dress tied at the waist with a wide belt of the same colour. This light clothing made the body it contained seem almost immaterial. She kneaded her fingers, still wet and a little red, as she looked at me. I had the disturbing thought that I didn't know much about her. I could describe every minute of her days, yet I had no access to her secret thoughts. There were times when I felt truly alone on earth.

"You know Cécile?" she finally asked.

"Well... no, not really."

"So which Cécile are you asking me about?"

Not daring to mention our night-time meeting in front of the refrigerator, I evoked the daytime Cécile. "I was with Bagatelle in the old high-school courtyard, and a woman who told me her name was Cécile came and talked to me."

"And?"

"She knew my name, and she said she was a friend of yours."

"A friend."

Mum seemed to struggle briefly against an invisible current of air. She took her handkerchief from her apron and blew her nose gently into it. Before folding it, she examined it closely, as if it might reveal some part of the mystery of her being.

"What did you talk about?" she asked, sniffing.

"Nothing much... stuff about birds... because of my dove."

"She didn't say anything about me?"

"No. I showed her my drawing and she chatted to me for a bit... Then she left. Do you know her?"

"Cécile... is a friend."

"From before?"

By that, I meant before her marriage to Dad and her move to the farm.

"No. She works at the post office in Possens."

"Is that where you see her? When you go to the post office?"

"Yes. That's where I met her."

"But what do you do together? I got the feeling that she..."

I stopped, because Mum suddenly came and sat down at the table opposite me, which she never did. I glanced anxiously at the potatoes frying in the cast-iron pan on the stove. Mum had two tiny wrinkles on each side of her mouth, barely even shadows, that descended towards her chin and were visible even when she smiled. These delicate folds of skin formed two unique little crescents, and they pointed up at her eyes as she said: "Cécile is an amazing girl. She's different. She has an interesting view on everything. We talk... and sometimes we spend a whole afternoon together."

"Why can't she come round to our place for once?"

"But..."

Mum hesitated. I felt a pang of guilt at employing a stratagem that might force her to lie to me. I did my best to let her off the hook. "It doesn't matter. It's not important. As long as you get along with her!"

"She does me good. You know..."

She stretched out her hand. I reached out with the tips of my fingers. Between the dishes and the coffee-pot, our fingers brushed.

"You're a big boy now."

It was a statement of fact, and I could understand why she saw me that way. At that time, I was devoting a lot of my energy – albeit in a somewhat erratic fashion – to trying to look like an adult. Still, I couldn't entirely stifle the little voice inside me that wanted to shout out in denial.

"You can understand certain things. Life isn't always easy. Day after day after day..."

"I understand."

"Cécile does me good. It's been going on since..."

She stopped to listen to the floorboards as they bent under the weight of Dad's steps in the hallway. It was already half past seven. She got up and returned to the position she'd occupied in front of her pans before our little tête-à-tête. Against our will, we had been drawn back within our familiar environment.

Opposite me, his napkin tucked into the neck of his shirt, Dad held his bowl of milky coffee between his thick, slightly hooked thumbs. Years of milking had formed a calloused ridge that doubled the size of his knuckles. The muscles of his forearms, hypertrophied from countless repetitions of the same movement, made him look like Popeye after a can of spinach. Rudy stolidly went about consuming his *rösti*, as usual misjudging the relationship between the capacity of his mouth and the matter at the end of his fork. He scattered pieces of potato far and wide, which he then carefully gathered together, so that in the end he consumed almost as much from the table as from his plate.

Mum, who was again wearing her neutral, unsmiling face, served us, carefully avoiding my gaze. Having been briefly catapulted outside of time, we had now resumed our normal life, which only ever flows in one direction.

Before going out, I went upstairs to snoop around the guest room, so called even though no guest to my knowledge had ever slept there. It was mostly used for storage. Unheated, and full of decrepit furniture, old lamps and piled-up crates that gave off a strange smell, it didn't seem part of the house. I was intrigued by these objects that had never had a place in the inhabited rooms. I preferred them. They hadn't been worn out by familiarity. They had another life. The guest room also contained a small bookcase with the only books we owned: a few, lavishly illustrated albums of the countries of the world, that we had sent off for after saving up tokens on jars of jam or chocolate boxes. I would leaf through them, lingering over the carefully arranged, clichéd tableaux, and wonder if there was anywhere on earth as untidy and uninteresting as our village.

The bed had been stripped. Someone had slept there. The creased yellow quilt had been put back in place, but it was folded over in a new way. I flared my nostrils as I pressed my nose against the blanket. There was no intoxicating scent of patchouli above the lifeless smell of the dust imprisoned in its fibres. Cécile had not spent the night in this room.

* * *

Outside, the sky was hard as cardboard, as though any bird that flew through it might tear it in half. My dove was sitting numbly on my shoulder, and I stayed as still as possible so as not to make it fall over. If that happened, it would crash painfully onto its side, then frantically beat its wings to regain a standing position. Clumsy and trembling, it would remain for a while in a state of shock, its heart on the verge of exploding, its eyes bulging even further out of its head.

The distant hum of the village tractors on the roads merged in a uniform mass, like a vast drop suspended over the fields. I knew all the farmers, and could say with absolute certainty who was driving the red spot in the east or the blue spot in the west, both followed by a long line of dust. No vehicle strayed from the fixed route that led to its parcel of land. They never crossed paths.

Rudy entered the yard at a run, dangling the empty watering can, with Sheriff barking angrily at his heels. When they spotted me, they instantly changed course to head in my direction.

"Rudy! You shouldn't water Sheriff if he's just sleeping! Only if he's fainted!" Rudy didn't seem to fully understand this distinction, but the drenched Sheriff, grateful for my intervention, came over with his head lowered to claim some stroking.

It was still early, but the day was already showing clear signs that it was going to be different. Bagatelle's stable was empty. Her rope, almost disintegrated with age, hung loosely on the hook. She would have had to employ only a minimum amount of force to free herself. I kicked the bulges in the hay to locate my grandfather, scattering the dry wisps and stems until a loud "Ow! That's not nice!" told me I had found the right spot.

"Wake up! Bagatelle has run away!"

He got up slowly, as if it took a conscious effort to assemble his jumbled bones into a working skeleton. Once on his feet, he looked around him and carefully wiped off all the straw clinging to his clothes. It annoyed me that he took so long to verify my news with his own eyes.

"It's not possible," he muttered.

"Uh – yes! Can't you see? She isn't here!"

"I can see, Gus, but..."

"Where is she? I can't believe it. Every morning I practically have to kick her before she even moves one ear."

"She's gone out."

"Yes! That's what I'm saying!'

"Let's go and have a look. She might not have gone far."

I followed my grandfather onto the grassy strip that overlooked the rocky slope leading to the main road. We scanned the horizon, without success. My grandfather got out the crumpled pack of fags he'd been lying on all night. He took out a twisted cigarette and straightened it with trembling fingers before lighting up. He smoked over fifteen packs a week, recording in a little blue spiral notebook his tobacco consumption, which he calculated by length. One cigarette measured fourteen centimetres, and he would announce proudly at the end of each year that he had surpassed the one kilometre mark.

We stood there sheepishly, trying to understand how old horses could simply disappear without a trace, when our tractor suddenly came into view. It zoomed at top speed past the farm belonging to the Grins. I had noticed how Dad stepped on the accelerator whenever he came within sight of the property of these fat land-grabbers, who, instead of sticking like other people to their own patch, bought up everything they could, even fields that had always belonged to the commune, in order to exploit a few acres more. The Grins were proof that the era was over when small landowners could raise themselves up to the rank of gentry by dint of hard work alone.

Dad stopped. The tractor's throbbing engine, cramped beneath the long bonnet, sent staccato shivers running through the entire machine. On his tiny seat between the two huge, motionless wheels, holding the steering wheel, Dad vibrated with the rest of the tractor.

"What... are... you... you... doing... there... there?" he shouted.

"Bagatelle has disappeared. She left last night!"

"Well? You... have to... find her!" he replied, addressing me.

"Okay!"

"Go... on! She might... cause an... accident..."

"Okay, okay! I'm going."

"I'm... counting... on... you!" he shouted again, before moving off, re-balancing the forces at work within the machine and putting an end to its hectic shuddering.

As I walked away, I turned back to glance at my grandfather. He was looking in my direction through the smoke of his filterless Jobs, but he didn't see me. I imagined that he spent his time thinking about time – time past and the time that was left to him – though probably neither was substantial enough to really hold his interest. When I reached the bend in the road, he was still there on the knoll in front of the stable, in exactly the same position, and he seemed to blend into the posts that edged the meadows behind him.

It was easy to track Bagatelle from the elegant piles of manure she had left behind her. Their regular spacing suggested she had been walking at an unhurried, constant pace. I followed them through the village, peering into yards and gardens, but without finding her. Neither was she grazing in the shade of the linden in front of the old high school, the outermost limit of our usual daily walks. The pyramids of smoking balls, each with its own little tornado of flies, continued in a straight line towards the forest. I was on the path leading to the reservoir when Madeleine called out to me. She was running behind me to catch up.

"Gus! Gus! Wait for me! Where are you going? What's that bird on your shoulder?"

Maddie, a girl my age, was special and I didn't try to understand why. I only knew she must like me, because she often sought my company. Dad told me much later that she was the illegitimate child of a village boy who had slept with a girl engaged to someone else. The girl had married her fiancé because the families had long agreed on it. Madeleine knew she had two fathers, one under the same roof, the second under another not far away. Always alone, she seemed to have made no firm connections on this earth, like those nomad cats that go from farm to farm, looking for something they can never find. She often hung around the village doing nothing, which gave her numerous opportunities to meet me.

We walked along the high ridge that jutted out over the plain, gazing down at the panorama of burnt fields, before we arrived at the promontory known ironically by locals as the "Susten", after the famous mountain pass.

"It's a dove."

"A dove? Show me! Show me! I've never seen one."

Madeleine pressed up against me, her leg touching mine, the tips of her breasts like two little leather buttons against my arm. I didn't object. It was just her way.

"Your dove is weird. It looks like something disgusting happened to its bottom."

She began to stroke the bird's head and wings, then its bare rump, performing a careful examination as it perched on my shoulder. She was standing very close. I was a little nervous of her handling my dove. I had seen her shift in an instant from the most sugary tenderness to the worst kind of cruelty towards animals.

"That's its tail, Maddie. Its tail has lost its feathers."

"Really?" she asked, surprised.

"That's why it can't fly anymore."

"Poor thing!"

"Yeah."

"Is it sick?"

"I don't think so."

She slid her fingers around my bird's appendage.

"It's red. And full of prickles!"

"That's the feathers growing back."

"Then will it be able to fly again?"

"Yeah."

Her mouth hanging slightly open, Madeleine seemed to be transfixed by something mysterious over my shoulder. A shadow passed over the curved, white protuberance of her forehead. I turned around to look for the cause of her stupefied expression, before realising that she was just staring into empty space, thinking what to say next.

"When?" she finally asked.

"Some day. I dunno."

"Then it will leave."

"What?"

I had not yet come so brutally face to face with this prospect.

"I don't think so. It wouldn't know where to go. It's a pet. It's grown attached to me."

Maddie pressed a little more against my legs, and looked straight in my eyes. On the surface of her irises were multiple, changing forms, all of them tinted by her loneliness.

"What are you doing here anyway?"

"I'm looking for Bagatelle. She..."

"Bagatelle?"

"Yes."

"Your horse?"

"Yes."

"I think I saw her... just down there. Near the river."

She pointed. I saw a tiny, dark spot in front of the majestic line of tall maples that separated the ravine leading down to the river from a field that had once belonged to us. It was where my grandfather had planted wooden stakes to create an enclosure, but the stakes hadn't been properly treated and had still contained enough tree-life to send out roots in conquest of the underground. In the spring, they were covered with branches and leaves. Anni had dug up half of them to give the others room to realise their full tree nature. I liked that patch of land a lot.

Bagatelle didn't want to move. Maddie and I tried to lure her away with a bouquet of dandelions, then we shoved her from behind with all our weight. We whispered sweet nothings into her ears, then harsh words, all to no avail. With her eyelids closed, Bagatelle obstinately kept her head down. She was breathing calmly, and occasionally her tail twitched.

We sat down in the field to ponder the situation. From time to time we heard a noise like a sheet of paper being crumpled, and turned to look behind us, but it was just the grass. It was crackling in the sun, its brittle blades bending and snapping under the weight of insects looking for a place to rest.

"It seems like she's thinking," said Maddie.

"Yeah. I wonder what's going on in her head."

"Do you think she's unhappy?"

"No! Look – she's calm. Like she's asleep."

"It's just that when I think, it upsets me."

"What do you mean, it upsets you?"

Maddie fixed her large, blue eyes on mine. There was something out of place in her head that gave a special power to her gaze. She always looked as if she were coming out of a deep sleep.

"When I think, it's as if someone's talking to me. Someone else. Do you know what I mean? Telling me things I don't agree with."

Maddie pressed her whole body against me, resting her forehead on my shoulder. I looked at her thighs, so white and smooth they seemed not to be part of the rest of her brown, bony body. I slipped my arm around her waist, and for a long time we stayed motionless, like Bagatelle, who was slowly baking in the sun, indifferent to the flies that flew in and out of her nostrils in search of moisture. No girls could compare with my beautiful sister, who seemed to belong to a different race. But I liked Maddie.

"She's drying out. The liquid inside her body is evaporating. Soon she'll be completely hollow..."

I shrugged.

"... or one morning you'll find her all shrivelled up, like an old piece of fruit."

Out of principle – because it was very hot, because it was Maddie – I agreed that it was possible.

* * *

"It's magnificent. She has chosen her place to die. We should leave her alone. We shouldn't move her. Animals have something in their head that's like a clock. It keeps time their whole life. It's never wrong. They know perfectly well when they're going to pass away. They understand it and it doesn't make them panic. They remain calm. They withdraw. They accept that their body is slowing down, growing tired, stopping..."

It was Cécile who had just spoken. Dad stared at her. His face tensed, as if he were on the point of a vigorous objection, but no sound came out of his mouth. He leaned over his soup, hoping to find peace among the leeks and potatoes. For once, Mum had joined us at the table. She was bewitched. Her eyes said, "What luck to be alive! So there *are* moments of grace, and with every season more happiness can be stored up!" Yet her hunched shoulders, her elbows pressed against her body, her controlled gestures – as if she were trying not to wake a monster lying at our feet – seemed to answer: "What's inside my head will never be compatible with the reality of this kitchen!" In her usual role of distant observer, Léa only smiled – but it was a smile of complicity.

Rudy was chewing enthusiastically, as if captivated by the implacable machinery of his jaws, which continued their mastications even when nothing remained in his mouth. He was gazing amorously at Cécile, captivated by the tiniest of her movements. He couldn't get over this miraculous presence. I knew what was going on inside his skull. He could not help but think of this stranger as his future wife, sent by a Providence whose ways would forever remain mysterious. From time to time he smiled, nodding his head with a knowing, blissful air.

"It's in the shade. The grass there is definitely less burnt. She's like those very old elephants who've lost their teeth. They leave the group. They look for a place with food that's more tender, so that they can end their lives without disturbing anyone," continued Cécile.

Dad, struck by a worrying thought, looked up from his bowl. "She'll be outdoors all night... What if she gets the idea to move somewhere else?"

"I tied her to the nearest tree. With a long rope."

He gave a nod of approval. "Hmm! I'll go and see her tomorrow morning."

"Our planet influences the lives of those it bears. Animals are very sensitive to manifestations of this sort. Before an earthquake, bees leave their hives. Ants run as far away as possible, carrying their eggs with them. They feel the telluric forces. Your horse has found a positive vibratory environment for its final moments."

Dad put his napkin down on the table and pushed his chair back to give himself a little room. He waved his hand in front of him to shoo away an imaginary swarm of insects. "I'll go and see her. Tomorrow morning before I go to the hen-house," he said to me.

"Okay."

"Maybe I can get her to move."

I knew that the possibility we would find Bagatelle dead in the meadow was making him anxious. Just digging a big hole and burying her on the spot was out of the question. We would have to drag her back up to the road with the tractor, then load her onto the slaughterhouse truck. The prospect of this inglorious end was preying on his mind.

"She could become an attraction, couldn't she? If she stays there for a few days?" asked Cécile.

Dad gave her a long stare, but she didn't back down. She went on smiling. She was wearing a low-necked, orangey tunic with shades of chestnut brown and a long necklace of metal and enamel plates that jiggled between her tanned breasts when she leaned forward to talk. Around her head was an Indian scarf, decorated with a few trinkets here and there. I watched as Dad's eyes seemed to transform into two big, round drops of water about to lose their spherical shape. The painful thought that he might find her beautiful and feel desire for her skimmed through me.

Mum sneezed violently. I had the impression that she had expectorated a parcel of brain into her handkerchief. She scrunched it up and quickly returned it to her apron, as if to dispose of unpleasant thoughts.

"Cécile has been working at the post office, at the Possens branch, ever since she started living alone," she said. "She left her husband a few years ago... he... well, it was a bad match." She turned to Cécile, who gave her a discreet nod, as if to say, "Go on! *Courage*! It'll be fine." It appeared that they had come to a prior agreement about what to say.

I felt my lips tense up involuntarily as I listened.

"Cécile lodges above the post office, in a separate room, a sort of little studio with a bathroom. It belongs to the couple who live in the flat next door. They set it up for a little extra income because their boy went off to do some training in town, to become a..."

Mum turned to Cécile.

"... a salesman," she said.

"That's it, a salesman... And... so now... their son... he couldn't find a job... has come back to live with his parents. But, well... he's settling in. I mean... he has a girlfriend. Cécile has to leave. And... I thought in the meantime she could come and live here. There's the guest room. We'd just have to get rid of the mess, give it a good clean..."

Léa, who until then had remained as indifferent to the conversation as she was to almost everything that didn't involve either her or music, now exclaimed, "But that's a great idea! Don't you think, Rudy?"

Rudy looked at my sister, not grasping what she wanted from him, a steady stream of soup connecting his mouth with the table.

Léa took his hand. "Rudy, don't you think it's a good idea for Cécile to come and stay here? To come and live in our house…"

Rudy screwed up his eyes in a knowing way, though probably he still hadn't understood anything. He smiled at my sister, then beamed at Cécile, which had the effect of breaking the semi-liquid thread that had tied him to the surface of the table. He continued to stare at her while he devoured his dunked bread, displaying the relentless work of his molars as well as most of the rest of the inside of his mouth. Vivid matrimonial ideas began to march around in his head. Mum gave Léa a meaningful look.

"It would be great for Mum to be able to spend some time with her friend, wouldn't it?" added Léa.

Dad shrugged as if say, "Why not?" while the rest of his motionless body seemed to ask, "What the hell is going on here?"

"It would only be for the summer. There are masses of things she could help me with… So, Jean, do you agree?"

I knew that this kind of request was a mere formality, having noticed long ago that he almost invariably said yes. I half-believed that he obeyed her because Mum's spirit was in touch with the divinity that protected our buildings, guaranteed the fertility of our land, and watched over our destiny; that it was only thanks to her that the house was still standing.

"I love animals," continued Cécile, as if this would help to convince Dad. "I have an excellent *rapport* with them. You can teach me how to milk."

Dad sighed. He respected animals. To treat them badly would be to debase his own humanity. But there was nothing emotional in the relationship.

"Well…"

"Please, Jean!"

"Fine. Yes, of course... She can stay as long as she likes. I'll put the furniture in the attic. You can help me, Gus."

"Okay. No problem."

Had my father glimpsed the wrath of our household gods if he were to refuse?

"Thank you!" said Mum, getting up to kiss his cheek. As she rose, she deliberately brushed against Cécile's bare arm, slowing down to prolong the contact.

Dad abandoned the kitchen, closing the door behind him. We heard his noisy passage along the narrow hallway, then his footsteps resounding in the yard. There was always something to do there. Rudy didn't follow. Certain vague thoughts were beginning to crystallise within him. He got up and took a red apple from the bowl on the big sideboard. Rubbing it with tender passion against his dirty jacket, he then used his hands and some spit to polish it up, before placing it delicately on Cécile's empty plate. She was as dumbfounded by the appearance of this shiny fruit as a botanist upon discovering a new species. Rudy remained standing right behind her, stiff and motionless as a major-domo.

"Thank you! That's very kind of you. I'll eat it later," she said.

It was not an ordinary apple; it was a gift. I knew how much it meant to Rudy. Any object that came under his gaze – a pebble, a radish, a farm tool – acquired for him a unique personality. Often he would stare at things for what seemed an eternity, with abnormal attention; he had an extraordinary ability to project himself into any element of his surroundings. It was his way of never being alone. The apple on the table was a part of himself, and he wanted nothing more in the world than to see Cécile bite into it.

"I feel as if you've adopted me!" said Cécile.

She took a bite, giving a rather forced smile as she chewed.

Rudy smiled at me knowingly. I felt bad as I contemplated the crazy dreams of this solitary man forever locked inside himself.

I was ashamed of myself, my sister, my mother. We were all powerless to prevent his disappointment. The song of the crickets, hidden in the brambles and bushes that snaked around the house, entered the kitchen through the open window. The sound was oddly shrill and sad in the dusk, as these insects, their wings atrophied since the beginning of time, fated to live all the blessed day at the bottom of dusty holes, began their night-long, starlit lamentation.

* * *

"For God's sake! Rudy! Stop messing around!"

I stared at Dad. In his anger, he had forgotten my presence, and almost screamed the words. We were awkwardly clad in our down-covered jumpsuits and our oversized boots, wet with sweat in the midst of the strangely listless and silent hens, who now moved only in slow-motion. Above our heads, the metal ceiling of the hen-house looked like a melting, white sky. For days, the heat inside had been inexorably climbing. The fans, designed for normal summers, were humming vigorously, but without lowering the temperature. Dad never swore, but Rudy had just put into the bag a not-quite-dead bird, which, plunged among the corpses of its fellows, had begun flapping its wings with frenzied desperation. Rudy was holding the hessian sack at arm's length, disconcerted by the convulsions within, yet determined not to let anything out.

"Idiot! Open the bag and take the poor animal out!"

Dad never called Rudy an idiot. He had always displayed a curious respect for this efficient work companion, who never needed to hear an order twice, who could perform the same gestures again and again with obsessive regularity and precision, who seemed, like the animals, the plants and the earth itself, connected to forces beyond human understanding. We had just witnessed a disturbing scene: a cluster of hens, driven to cannibalism, had been pecking away at a bloodless carcass, extracting shreds of flesh which they devoured quickly, heads back, as if swallowing a long worm. Dad had scattered them with a few kicks. Most of the dead birds were eyeless and mutilated, their de-feathered parts covered with deep holes.

Dad tore the bag from Rudy. He opened it quickly and took hold of the still-living hen, twisting its neck with a single jerk of his wrist, before placing it gently back inside.

"Here, take the bag back. From now on, only pick up the dead ones!"

For some days, Rudy hadn't been himself. He was no longer able to give his wholehearted attention to the things around him. Whenever he glimpsed Cécile – at a window, in the garden or talking with Mum in front of the house – he would cease all activity and remain standing as if turned to stone. His blissful smile told me all too clearly that he was imagining the intimate future moments that he and his promised one would share together. Among his possessions was a bottle of vetiver essential oil. He had started to make immoderate use of this – with the result that the animals in the barn had become unusually nervous in his presence – whilst also obsessively smoothing back with saliva the forelock that he had formerly allowed to fall forward onto his forehead. I was the only one who didn't tease him. Dad had complained more than once about having to follow him around to finish jobs that hadn't been done properly, which was very rare.

When we left the hen-house, we were abnormally distant from each other. Scattered and motionless, we were confined within our own mental spaces, powerless to escape the haunting, white-hot curse of the sun. I knew that others before us had experienced this sensation: adventurers who had survived a thousand deadly dangers; explorers who had found a way out of the poisonous jungle after battling wild animals, traps and hostile natives; Texas rangers who, after a mad, stampeding flight from pursuers shooting at their backs, could finally catch their breath in the shelter of a large rock. Such people found it hard to regain their balance. They too were unable to dislodge the fear in the pit of their stomachs. Generally, after a long period of silence, a member of the group would say something commonplace, and normal existence would resume its course.

We were busy tying a rope around the bags in the trailer, when we heard a horn sound out, then again, and again, like the raucous cries of a wounded animal. We climbed onto the hillock that overlooked the road. Cécile's car had pulled up on the grassy border, the engine still running. She was with Mum. The two women were leaning against the doors, looking in our direction. When they saw us, they waved. We waved back.

"We... ing... to..."

"Louder! We can't hear you!" shouted Dad.

"We... ing... ee..."

Cécile stepped forward to take over from my mother.

"Ee... ing... ter..."

Dad shrugged. Without taking his eyes off them, he asked me: "Did you understand anything?"

"Nothing."

Mum was in a close-fitting white dress that reached mid-thigh. From where we were, she looked like someone else; someone who looked like her, and moved like her, but might have been a happy young holiday-maker. Dad gave a slow, exaggerated shrug to signify that their voices hadn't reached us through the thin, dry air. Cécile whispered something in Mum's ear. She laughed and shook her head. Then Cécile half-disappeared into the car to re-emerge with a large sheet of paper that she placed on the bonnet. She and Mum bent over it as if to study a road map. All became clear when they each grasped one end, displaying it like a banner. It read: "WE'RE GOING INTO TOWN. BACK TONIGHT. AROUND SEVEN O'CLOCK."

We drove home at high speed on the cement paths that divided the fields. The wheels of our old Toyota and its trailer, raising behind us a line of dust as clear as a pen-stroke, seemed to be grinding up the solid ground. His neck muscles tensed, Dad gripped the steering wheel as though the wind that rushed through the four open windows might push us off the road if he relaxed for a single instant.

He must have been thinking of Cécile's red Renault 5, heading in the opposite direction, into town. I gazed at the featureless sky above us, staring at a random point in the pale blue, near-white expanse, and for a few seconds I had the strange feeling that we were standing still.

Mum and Dad didn't talk much. Or maybe they did, in the bedroom? The only physical expressions of tenderness between them that I could remember were when Dad took Mum by her hand and pulled her to him quickly in a kind of ballet move. She would lower her eyes as he gave her a kiss behind the ear, a particularly touching spot, pale and rounded like a shell. She would then detach herself from him, pretending to fall backwards, and he would hold out his arm with a graceful gesture, as if to prevent her from falling.

With our load of dead hens still in the trailer, we made a detour by the reservoir because Dad wanted to see Bagatelle.

I showed him the place. Leaving the Toyota on the path above us, we descended slowly towards the hollow where our old horse stood, the dry grass stems snapping under our feet. She hadn't moved a millimetre. Dad walked around the old mare, inspected her as if he were looking for a tear in her coat, rubbed her nose for a long time, patted her a few times to chase away the horseflies gorging themselves on this inexhaustible source of fresh blood. At a loss in the face of such indifference, he shook his head, then tugged on the rope to check my handiwork from the day before.

"You did well to tie her up."

Rudy found a few dandelions, shrivelled but still with a trace of green, and held them in front of Bagatelle's mouth. Her lips didn't move. He looked at Dad as if he might be able to do something about it.

A strange smell drifted over from the large maples.

"Do you smell tobacco?"

"Yeah."

"It's coming from the forest."

I set off toward the trees. From behind some bushes, a faint, blue plume of smoke rose into the air.

"There's someone there!"

Suddenly my grandfather rose up. He was covered in twigs and seeds, which he brushed off with the back of his hand. All the trees were already laden with their autumn fruit, as if the year were going by in fast-forward.

"What are you doing there?"

"It's not so hot under my maples. It's not a bad spot."

"Did you sleep here?

"It's not uncomfortable. It's no harder than the stable floor."

"Were you lonely without Bagatelle?"

"Now hold on a minute, don't start thinking..."

Dad waved us over.

Anni lifted his feet over the undergrowth, making a wheeling motion with his arms as he walked. The joints of his bony body seemed reluctant to perform the actions he was asking of them, and he staggered a little, as if the ground beneath his feet were unstable. Finally, he managed to coax a more or less normal gait from his rusty limbs.

"What's going on, Anni? What about Rose? What if she doesn't find you at home?"

"It happens all the time. She knows I'm never far away. Don't worry about it."

Dad stared at his father for a long time. He was unable to get angry with this person who had given him both life and the farm, especially when all that was left of him was skin and bone. Anni took a twisted cigarette from his pocket with his equally misshapen fingers, and lit it with some difficulty.

"You're going to start a fire with your fags," said Dad. "She still hasn't moved," he added.

"Doesn't surprise me. She's always been a stubborn mare. Lazy and stubborn. Always had to be the one to decide... Horses are like that. It's part of their nature... *Du bisch di Schönschti. Du bisch starch, du bhaltisch dy Platz unter üs!*[1] murmured Anni, patting Bagatelle's sides as if to get rid of the dust.

"Her ears are drooping," said Dad.

"It's because she's not concerned about anything anymore. She's resigned."

"All right, we'll leave her there. It must be the arthritis. She's in too much pain. Or maybe everything just seized up."

"It's possible. She wants to die standing up. Not on her knees,

1 You're a real beauty. You're strong, you'll keep your place among us!

not lying down, but standing up – and outdoors," concluded my grandfather, in a strange, hushed tone of voice, as though he were confiding something of a deeply personal nature.

V

How exhausting was that summer of 1976, always beating down on our heads!

We'd arrived home late in the morning. After a little reading and drawing, I had sat down on the garden wall, with my bird on my shoulder. The light died with agonising slowness, until an immense, warm shadow finally enveloped the mass of our house. Everything drew closer together and became more intimate within the perimeter marked by the hulks of the buildings, the kitchen-garden wall and the barbed-wire fences. The sun had left behind it a lava-like deposit of heat that continued to weigh on the earth. My dove rested, its eyes half-closed, steeped in the ancestral dignity of birds, for whom everything is boring apart from whirling through the air.

Sheriff crossed the yard gingerly, scrutinising the sky. The last few days, he had seemed anxious, as if he were expecting a cold rain to shower down on his head at any moment. He carefully avoided the watering can beside his kennel, even baring his fangs to warn off this cunning enemy.

Sounds of anger drifted over from the barn. Above the hum of the machines and the crackle of the dusty old radio Dad used to create a calm, musical environment during milking, variations on the theme of "shit," "fuck," and "damn" rang out. These curses were answered by the metallic din made by the cows' hooves, as they jostled and shoved, before at last coming to a standstill, stamping the ground angrily.

Cécile and Mum were strolling through the vegetable garden, arms around each other's waists. They were chatting, with Cécile doing most of the talking. My mother listened as she expertly handled the watering hose. From time to time, they exchanged little laughs that were quickly stifled, and when they bent down to inspect a row or pick a tomato or a cucumber, I had the impression they had a lot to say to the vegetables too. Rudy, who had finished his work in the barn, walked by, his lock of hair slicked to his forehead. Paying me no attention, he marched to join them with energetic strides that betrayed his excitement. All of a sudden, my dove emerged from its torpor. It hopped and jumped as if an electric current were shooting through its body, then turned around two or three times before finally calming down. Perhaps its former owner, the magician, had worn the same vetiver perfume as Rudy when he went onstage.

Rudy had begun to follow Cécile wherever she went. I looked at the greasy moon. It hung heavily over the trees, as though it wanted to make its own contribution to the oppressive heat.

"Rudy! Stop!"

Mum was over by the water tap, opening and closing it to regulate the flow into the hose. In the middle of the garden, Rudy grabbed Cécile and pressed himself against her. Still holding the hose, she was trying to free herself, crying out:

"Stop it! Get your hands off me! Shit! You're hurting me!"

She struggled, hitting him with the fists of her free arm wherever she could reach – on his head, his back, his neck – but Rudy wasn't remotely bothered by these rough caresses, as they must have seemed. She didn't have a chance. Usually gentle and easy-going, Rudy was nevertheless endowed with almost super-human strength. Only a single idea occupied his skull at any one time, so that there was nothing to restrain the pure power of his muscles, forged by daily labour. This captive strength, always ready to free itself, helped to explain the instinctive fear Rudy inspired in some people.

"Pervert! Take your hands off me! Filthy pig!"

There were tears of rage in Cécile's voice, but Rudy was not going to give up easily. He knew that letting go would immediately break the spell.

Mum turned the water up to maximum and ran towards them, shouting as I had never heard her shout: "Let her go! Rudy! Let her go!"

She aimed the jet at Rudy's back. Sprays of water, gleaming in the moonlight, rose towards the sky. Little by little, under the effect of the cold shower, and because Mum had over him the unquestioned authority of a mother over a child, he began to let go. Cécile finally managed to shove him back and free herself. Trapped within an enormous cage of water, Rudy fell onto his back in the midst of the leeks. Mum went calmly to turn off the tap, then returned to help Cécile re-adjust her opened blouse as well as she could, tenderly caressing the back of her neck and whispering in her ear what must have been words of comfort.

Rudy stayed on the ground. I was ashamed. Mum too, perhaps, because she went to help him to his feet. She gave him a harsh dressing-down to put him in his place, before Cécile made a gesture of reconciliation. Covered in mud, his head full of something heavy that made his tearless face look swollen, Rudy walked past me to take refuge in his bedroom. He no longer smelled of essence of vetiver, only of earth and solitude. I watched him slink away like an outcast, with no one to console him, and I hated those two women.

* * *

Some instinct of survival had pulled me violently out of sleep. I was bathed in sweat, as though plunged in a tub of warm water, and stars danced before my eyes. I slowly came to, with an anguished sense of having lost something for ever, a feeling that even the coloured spines of my cartoon albums, arranged neatly in order of publication on my shelves, couldn't dispel. The window was open onto an infinite sky, empty and menacing; a black rectangle that seemed on the point of sucking up the matter of my body as though it were as fluid as water. My dove wasn't on its perch. All of a sudden, I felt certain that it had been pulled into that realm of darkness.

I leaned out of the window, resting my hands on the sill. My dove's unhappy attempt at night flight had ended with a fall into our yard. The moon illuminated the bird with strange clarity, as it trembled between two large, round paving stones; it was as though the dead star had sent out a special ray of light, brighter than all the others, to fall exactly upon it. It looked as smooth and brilliant as a bird from the first days of Creation. Every predator in the neighbourhood must have been watching, held back only by the suspicion that prey offered in this way, with its very own robes of light, must be a trap.

"Whoa! Slow down! Where are you rushing off to?"

I had to halt my mad flight down the stairs as I came up against the mass of Dad, blocking the way, his shoulders touching the walls. He too was on the way down, and as he turned, I caught a whiff of straw, rancid milk and sweat. His face was a little blurred. The door to the little guest room was open. He had slept there!

He looked exhausted, as if he was carrying the entire house on his back, to try to move it to a more favourable spot.

"My bird went out of the window!"

"Auguste..." sighed Dad.

"It fell out... I have to go and get it!"

"A bird that can't fly..."

"I don't want it to get caught..."

"You should leave it... A bird without a tail... It wanted to kill itself, that's all."

"Dad... did you sleep in the little room?"

His body seemed to grow larger, and the passage narrower. "Mind your own fucking business," he growled.

"But..."

"Shut your mouth!"

"Okay, okay!"

I felt that he might easily punch me, just like that, for nothing. It was an odd sensation when he placed his back against the wall to let me pass. I went by in silence, brushing against the metal of his belt, afraid he would grab me suddenly by the neck and pick me up like the dying chicken in Rudy's sack, the one whose neck he had broken. I breathed the outside air with relief, suddenly aware of the still vastness of the night above my small body. My dove hadn't budged. It quivered in the hollow of my hands when I stroked the top of its head. I was sure now that it had accepted me as its rightful owner.

Dad crossed the yard slowly, with his head low, as if he had decided once and for all that he would carry on living just as calmly as he had always done.

* * *

Maddie often came and sat next to me on the school bus. As she passed down the narrow aisle, the other children would avoid meeting her eyes, and begin to talk with false animation. They would put their bags on the free seats, so as not to have to spend time with her during this journey through landscapes so familiar that they had long since lost all interest. Alone in my corner seat, I would read my magazines, with Maddie cuddled up against me. From time to time, she would glance at me in silence. We were like an old couple pickled in decades of collusion, no longer needing to exchange anything, least of all words.

Perhaps the reason I didn't feel uncomfortable in Maddie's presence was that she had once shown me how to resuscitate drowned flies. We were standing in front of the stable door. Insects were pouring out, in a state of intoxication as they emerged from shit-smelling darkness into the sunlit, infinite azure. Maddie intercepted them with what must once have been a milk-skimming net, and trapped them in a large glass jar. When the harvest was over, and twenty or so flies swarmed in confusion inside, she opened the lid a fraction and slowly filled it with water, before shaking it to create a violent storm. The flies waggled their feet uselessly, to try to free themselves from the fluid that sucked them towards death. "Look!" said Maddie urgently, moving her face within a centimetre of mine. This was her way of strengthening her argument, while at the same time making any escape impossible. Later, I learned that she had bad eyesight and that, out of negligence or meanness, her parents never bought her glasses. "Look!" she said. "They're pretending to be dead." She took out a fly and placed it on a sheet of newspaper sprinkled with a thick layer of salt. At this contact, the fly at once began to roll frantically over and over, before stretching itself out segment by segment, and at last flying vertically upwards away from this earthly horror. After the same rough awakening, all the captured flies lit off like rockets, in various directions, but always in a straight line, so that a few crashed violently into the nearest obstacle, this time falling dead for real.

One day, I was hanging about near the old high school with my sketchbook, caught in a trance-like state of lethargy, when Maddie, seemingly trying to break free of the same spell, persuaded me to walk with her through the fields to the stream. Its ancient, wooded banks, cut deep into the earth, might still hold a little coolness and shade despite the angry sun, she said.

"Do you recognise it?"

"Eh?"

"Can you hear the tune?"

"What are you talking about? What tune?"

We were crushing the heat-shrivelled grass beneath our feet. In some places, it had completely disappeared, to reveal a black, smooth, beaten earth that looked as if it had been slow-roasted. Beside me, Maddie was moving forward in an odd way. Lifting her right leg very high, she would bring it down forcefully on the hard ground, then do the same with her left leg. The rhythm had more in common with a tribal dance than with normal walking. It reminded me of island-dwelling cannibals, covered in war-paint and waving their totems around some immense fire, before setting off, light at heart, to battle.

"My feet are making music."

She made five or six leaps, as if she were treading on hot coals. The dry grass under our feet was like crackling paper, and each one of her steps, according to how much force she used, and exactly how she set her foot down, produced its own sound, drum-like or high-pitched, long or short, solemn or frivolous.

"Do you recognise the song?"

"No. Not really..."

"*Oh, What A Night*!"

"Eh? What night?"

She repeated the same sequence of leaps, her knees almost reaching to her chin, before concluding, with five or six feverish little steps, while chanting, "Oh, what a night. I felt a rush like a rolling bolt of thunder..." She looked at me, out of breath, her eyes wide: "It's *The Four Seasons*!"

"Oh yeah. That's it... You've got it!"

Full of gratitude, she rubbed up against me, her hair tickling my face.

The trees clinging to the slope along the path that snaked down towards the river, with their curled-up leaves, scarcely deflected the rays of the sun. But as we neared the bottom of the valley, a heavy, flat shade came over us, offering little relief. The stream hadn't dried out. It was flowing silently, the pebbles visible under the water, as brilliant and smooth as agates. Maddie pulled up her skirt and jumped into the middle of the current, splashing wildly in all directions, all music-making forgotten.

"Come on! Let's walk along the river. We can go to the pool under the waterfall."

Fifty metres downstream, surrounded by humps of earth covered with leafy shrubs, a thin flow of water filled a slightly deeper section of the stream, from the centre of which rose a flat rock. Wet to the tops of our thighs, we climbed onto it and sat down. The coolness of the river, reflected by the overhanging branches of the trees, enfolded us. A few river plants shaped like large, flared ears – we called them wild ginger – seemed to have miraculously escaped the heat wave. We shivered with pleasure. We felt like Robinson Crusoe on his island, survivors far from all other humans. I wished I had brought along my bird. Trapped beneath its quilt of feathers, it would have appreciated this light, cool air.

Maddie snuggled up to me, slipping her arm around my waist. Her ribcage rose and fell against my torso. She had a slightly rough way about her; there was a nervous energy and a bluntness in her movements and gestures, a self-confident way of walking and running that reminded you of a boy. Her adolescent body seemed to be inhabited by a small, virile, stubborn being. I found its presence very reassuring. I also liked Maddie's smell. I will always associate her with the delicate odour of grass fermenting in the sun.

"I hear voices."

"Hmm?"

"Voices. In the wood... Can you hear?"

I strained my ears for a sound beyond that of the diminutive waterfall, like a tap slowly filling a sink.

"People are coming."

"Uh-huh."

"The voices are getting closer."

Disentangling our arms and legs, we climbed down from our rock. Thighs stinging from the cold, we hurried through the water towards the bank, then pulled ourselves a few metres up the steep slope, clinging to branches, before slipping behind a trunk whose base, surrounded by wild ginger, hid us perfectly. Maddie took my hand in hers. I let her, only to regret it a moment later when Mum and Cécile came into view, arm in arm by the river's edge, in the very spot where we had been a minute before. They scanned their surroundings to check they were alone, then examined the ground and the bank. When they discovered our tracks, they turned their attentions to the opposite shore, thinking we must have crossed the ford. I hunched deeper behind our hiding place, crushing the over-inquisitive Maddie against the trunk.

"Ow! Who is it?"

"I... I dunno."

Satisfied they were alone, their movements became freer and more relaxed. Cécile was the first to take off her dress, drawing it over her head in a single, fluid motion that seemed to make it magically disappear. She removed her underwear and crumpled it into a ball, while Mum stood motionless in front of her. Cécile drew Mum tightly to her naked body and kissed her on the mouth for a long time, a very long time. Then she grasped the two straps of her dress, the same little blue dress Mum often wore at breakfast time, and slid them down her arms...

"Isn't that your mother? The small one?"

"Shut up!"

"Who's that with her? Oh wow! Oh wow!"

"Shut up! Shut up! Shut your mouth, or else!"

"But..."

"Come on! We're getting out of here."

We climbed up the bank, emerging into the treeless fields. From here, we had to make a wide detour to go back to the village; it was uphill too, which made it seem even longer. The concrete of the path was burning hot. With each step, the heat shot up through my body and jolted into my skull. Maddie walked two metres behind, annoyed by this brutal expulsion from our gentle, shaded, watery paradise. She dragged her feet, kicking pebbles in my direction. My head was full of the loud splashes and the laughter of the bathers behind us as we fled. Maddie understood nothing. She was like some kind of small animal, dumb and contemptible. *Go back to your hole*, I thought as we parted without a word at the crossroads near the dried-up fountain.

* * *

Dad was sitting at the end of the table. He looked as if he didn't have enough air to function normally. When he exerted himself, for example by lifting a heavy sack of feed, his creased, red face would metamorphose into a strange landscape of hollows and humps. Now, he was at rest. Staring straight ahead, he seemed to want nothing more than to reduce the world to the space between his nose and the coffee-pot on the stove. Yet even a reality of these shrunken proportions was too large for comfort.

"Music is breath. Nature breathes. The water of the river swirling around the rocks breathes. The wood that creaks with the changes of weather breathes. The earth becomes wet, dries out, closes, opens up, breathes... It's an exchange, always an exchange between the inside and the outside... We don't just breathe with our lungs. We breathe with our skin too, with our bones... with everything! We're much more permeable than we think. Out... in... out... in... That's the real rhythm of the world. That's why each inhalation is... is like a prayer... and music is a cosmic breath... a breath that links us to the earth, to the sun, to the moon... the stars emit pulsations because their temperatures vary... pulsations that are acoustic waves, that can actually be heard by the human ear."

Every time Cécile turned towards Léa or Mum, her necklace of coloured pearls and shells, with its swirling orifices shaped like big nostrils, moved against her breasts, clinking against each other. This sound was alien to our kitchen. We were all acutely aware of it, perhaps even more than we were of Cécile's words.

"Neil Armstrong had a recording of Dvořák with him during the Apollo mission. He was listening to the New World Symphony before he set foot on the moon," said my sister.

"That's crazy," replied Mum, a bit lamely.

Cécile was sitting abnormally close to her. There was a lot of room around our big table, but their chairs were almost touching.

Each time they moved, their shoulders rubbed against each other, and they would remain stuck together for a few seconds by the sweat of their naked skin, as if to permit the exchange of some mysterious fluid.

"The spring that gurgles and breathes, the grain that cracks and whose seed makes a passage for itself to the open air, the tree that contracts its leaves, then dilates them when the wind cools down... that's what it means to be natural. A lot of people are shrivelled inside... closed up... their vital organs are shrunken... their lungs become stiff and dry... the body is no longer illuminated ... it's not open ... it becomes coated with miasma. As if living were nothing special, just a necessary evil! That's because of unhappiness... Not feeling accepted by what surrounds us..."

Cécile looked at Dad, who ignored her. He was still absorbed in the space between himself and the coffee-pot.

"Good breathing calms the nerves, calms fears... It's like when wind blows on fire, scattering the ashes and reviving the flame that was suffocating underneath."

Dad emptied his glass in one gulp and turned his head away from all of us. There was a long moment of silence, during which I could hear the liquid descending into his stomach.

Mum and Cécile had cooked together that night. I remember it was a Berne speciality of dried beans, potatoes and bacon. It had, however, been adapted somewhat from the original, the beans being fresh, bright green and crunchy, the meat replaced by cubes of white cheese... Rudy grew even more focused on his plate than usual, inspecting each forkful in disbelief. From time to time, he would throw an angry glance in Cécile's direction, but she just kept on talking, and talking, and talking, while Rudy looked at her with the same expression of loathing he'd once given the sharp stone he'd finally found in his boots after it had been tormenting him all day.

Mum couldn't take her eyes off Cécile. Her fingers ran lightly over her cheeks as if she were re-acquainting herself with her own physiognomy. I had the strange impression that her face had become larger, and that with these discreet caresses she was attempting to soften and relax it even more. The sides of her nostrils, usually roughened and red, had rediscovered a lost freshness. I suddenly realised that she was no longer suffering from allergies, even though asthmatic allergies were an inseparable part of Mum. Perhaps the swim with Cécile in the river had cleaned out her sinuses. I hated the air that she breathed, because it was the air Cécile was breathing next to her.

Then Mum said, in a very clear voice: "I'm going to get a job."

She looked at Dad, who remained inscrutable, then at my sister, who smiled back in a way that gave me the unpleasant feeling that they'd already plotted this together. As if no one had heard, Mum repeated: "I'm going to get a job."

Dad had always refused to let her do any extra activities, even if they were only to "make ends meet", as she put it. For him, any occupation outside the farm was a distraction from what really mattered. There had been the motorway, whose distant roar you could sometimes hear on the westerly breeze; there had been the biscuit factory, where many children of the village had gone to work; there had been the new road, cutting the trip into town by almost half an hour. A web was weaving itself around our countryside. It was a web in which he didn't want us to get caught.

"I'm telling you I'm going to get a job!"

Dad slowly turned his head towards Mum, and we all watched this turning of his head as if it were a very special event of unprecedented importance.

He said nothing. Mum continued, in a voice that was a little less definite: "Cécile has found me a job at the post office. It's ideal for me... part-time. Three afternoons a week in Possens, the last shift at the counter... Sorting out the letters..."

Dad remained silent. Was I the only one who noticed the shudder that went through the taut skin of his forearms?

"The pay is pretty good," added Cécile.

"That's great!" my sister exclaimed. "You'll get to have new experiences, meet people..."

Dad got up slowly and gripped the edge of the table. Filling his lungs with air, he rushed at Cécile, flattening her against the wall and gripping her neck with both hands to throttle her. Mum, who had stepped aside to let him pass, hovered near the door, as if she might flee at any moment.

"Jean! Jean! Stop it! Stop it!" she shouted.

Rudy and I exchanged glances. He was very calm, his fork suspended in the air with its cargo of beans as green as the first shoots of spring. In his eyes was a malicious glint; it was the yellow glint of pleasure at a violent but liberating shock. He smiled at me. Was the glow in his eyes mirrored in my own?

"Jean! You're crazy! Stop it! Stop it! You'll kill her!"

That did, in fact, seem to be Dad's goal, and there could be no doubt he would succeed. He was possessed with a strength that was no longer his own.

"You bunch of idiots! What's wrong with you? Do something!"

My sister shoved my chair, slamming my head back against the wall, and leapt over me. She grabbed hold of Dad's back and pulled, but without managing to move him a centimetre. She was like a little carnivorous raptor clinging with its claws onto an enormous diplodocus.

"Dad! Stop! Let go!"

She shoved her knee into him again and again, pulled his hair, pummelled his sides with her fists. He continued methodically to strangle Cécile, whose short, hoarse breaths had started to sound like those of some tiny mammal. The shells around her neck were no longer clinking. All I could think was "Go! Go!" Not for a moment did I imagine the inevitable consequences of a murder in our kitchen: Cécile's lifeless body at our feet, Dad thrown into prison, our family broken up for ever. Instead, I savoured the panic in the eyes of our mother, as she stood there, powerless, voiceless, her mouth open, holding her cheeks as if to keep her head from exploding. I couldn't have cared less about Cécile; I was watching Mum's face, deformed by fear. She was only getting what she deserved. This horrible scene would sort everything out. She would finally understand. She would finally understand that we loved her more than anyone in the world. Above all, she would understand that I loved her more than that girl could ever love her. During those endless-seeming moments, I think I believed that Cécile would simply vanish from our lives, like the enemies my comic-strip heroes blasted out of existence. Jeering and mocking, Rudy was clearly of the same opinion.

"Fuck! Stop it! Dad! Let her go!"

Suddenly, Dad stepped back. He examined his hands. Cécile straightened up. Her face flushed, she looked at him incredulously, her mouth limp, her lips dead. Dad took a few more steps backwards, with Léa still hanging onto his back. The ordinary commotions of the outside world returned: a tractor rumbling in the distant fields, the indifferent hum of the refrigerator, the sizzling of insects on the lamp, the despairing song of the crickets. We were all there in that room, but it was as if none of us existed.

Dad left the kitchen unhurriedly and in silence, as he did every night. His mind was already on the chores waiting for him outside. Once the door was closed and the sound of his footsteps had faded away in the depths of the hallway, Mum threw herself into Cécile's arms, joined immediately by my sister, who embraced them as if she were trying to bring them even closer together. They repeated over and over reassuring little phrases – "Everything will be fine! Everything will be fine!" – like soft, magical incantations. After a while, Rudy followed Dad. Léa turned from stroking Mum's back to glance at me. Alone at the big table, I felt like an intruder. I stayed there for a minute, hollowed out, not crying because there was no one to witness my tears, before I too abandoned the scene.

VI

The next morning we ate in silence, as if nothing had happened, except that Mum wasn't there. She was still asleep in the bedroom above our heads, no doubt in the arms of Cécile.

The sky took on a weird colour. As the dawn slowly diluted the night, the air turned dirty-yellow. It was as if the sun had decided to travel millions of kilometres closer to the earth, to descend into the lower layers of our atmosphere, and dissolve there. Deep in the oven below, we continued to bake like biscuits. Rudy was sweating a lot, but only in certain places; his glands seemed to be unevenly distributed under his skin. Big drops streamed from his nose and his chin while his forehead, cheeks, and prominent cheekbones remained dry. From time to time, he would try to empty his overflowing pores with a downward swipe of his hand, which had left a vivid red stripe on his face.

We were in the car on the way to the hen-house. Dad hadn't opened his mouth. There was nothing to say. Speaking would only have deposited a useless layer of words on top of things. When reality showed its ugly side, when it refused to abide by the normal rules of fair play, Dad would just shove his fists into his pockets, and wait in silence for it to pass.

My dove, perched on my shoulder, was tense, braced against

the wind rushing in through the open windows as the car sped along. With every lurch, the bird's claws buried themselves in my flesh, and I held it tightly to stop it from being sucked outside. I could feel the hard bristles at its rump, announcing the imminent regrowth of its feathers.

Dad was very worried about the hens. The customer who was supposed to buy the whole lot was due to visit in two weeks, and the birds weren't getting any bigger. They ate their grain without putting on weight, their organisms exhausted by the struggle against the heat. The fans were functioning normally, but they weren't designed for an apocalyptic heat wave. Their motors, spinning at full throttle, as loudly as the engine of a Jumbo Jet, gave the impression that they were raising the temperature. The death rate was high. As we gathered up the ragged little bodies, the truth stared us in the face. Our investment was doomed. The sparse rows of survivors, their flesh as dry as if it were already cooked, could not possibly give us any profit. All we could do was save what could still be saved.

Rather than going straight to the hen-house, we made a detour to visit Bagatelle. We felt mysteriously drawn to her. Our old mare, who had once paced tirelessly up and down our fields, who had learned to recognise a few simple instructions that helped her pick her way between the delicate crops, had left her stable to die outside. Somehow this act had lodged her firmly at the forefront of our minds, even though none of us was quite sure why she'd done it.

I looked at Dad's hands on the steering wheel, which jumped at every irregularity in the road. The hands that had tried to strangle Cécile. Rudy was in the back, all his concentration on the shifting landscape. He would settle on a detail and track it with his eyes until it disappeared behind him. Then he would follow another one, until that too disappeared, so that he kept turning his head from side to side, his forehead pressed against the window.

I closed my eyes, and was engulfed by a vast nothingness, gradually losing all purpose as torpor vanquished every part of my body. The yellow sky, the yellow fields, the car splitting the yellow air on the yellow road... They were all unreal. The winter mornings, when the cold hardened the ground and squeezed things together. Dad's broad, bent back as he crossed the yard to begin the daily struggle. Mum, whose joints almost seemed to come apart when she tried to run. The windows in the roof of the barn, shrouded with dusty cobwebs that let though no light. Sheriff, resigned to his destiny, and yet afraid of everything. The doors of our house, always closed as if each room contained priceless treasures; doors that we spent our lives opening. Léa, whose awareness of her own beauty meant that she was always waiting for something marvellous and unexpected to happen. Spring, when the north wind blew, and everything became very cold and very colourful at the same time. Maddie's cool, indifferent-seeming hands when she touched me. My grandfather, Annibal, carrying the burden of his past, not knowing what to do with himself. Rudy, who was my friend because he never asked himself or the people around him difficult questions. Bagatelle, who had transformed herself into an ominous shadow in the middle of the fields... It was all inscribed forever in my nervous system. Groggy and half-asleep on the battered seat of our car, I felt that I'd been sentenced to lug around my entire reality with me at all times... No doubt this reality would only disappear when I died.

"What the hell is this?!"

The Toyota had stopped abruptly in the middle of nowhere.

Dad got out, slamming the door violently behind him. With his shoulders squared and his fists swinging, he set off towards the line of tractors parked in the burnt meadow. They looked like a procession of big grasshoppers. Dad knew their owners.

"It looks like something's going on."

"Yes."

"We'll go and have a look."

"Yes. We'll go and have a look," said Rudy, who was satisfying an urgent need to clean out his nose very thoroughly, a finger in each nostril. He was waiting for a reassuring sign before he would venture out of his quiet self-sufficiency into this rather unusual situation. I put my dove down on the headrest and climbed out of the car. Rudy followed. "We'll go and have a look. We'll go and have a look," he repeated, still trying to calm himself down before this encounter with the unknown.

Bagatelle hadn't moved from her spot below the road. I was relieved to see her silhouette, which had already acquired the status of a landmark. A small crowd had gathered around her. Anni was standing next to her old head. He seemed to be arguing with three men, arranged in a half-circle around him. Dad joined them.

"Hello, Jean!" they said, one after the other, as if they had made a prior agreement to echo each other.

Ignoring this greeting, Dad addressed Anni. "Is there a problem with Bagatelle?"

"No. She's just waiting," replied my grandfather. Then, in the ancestral language he reserved solely for his horse's ear, he whispered, *"Myni Schöni! Du bisch jitz alt, bald muesch du stärbe... Aber es git es Paradies... o für Ross."*[1]

---

1 "My beautiful one! You're old now, soon you'll have to die... But there is a paradise... even for horses."

Dad paid no attention to the other men. There was Dind, who owned thirty hectares and rented ten more; Pellaux, not far behind, with a big farm after a lucky marriage; Grin, whose ancestors had hauled themselves over the years into the ranks of the gentry. It was several days since Dad had seen anyone outside the family. He seemed to have decided that only objects and animals were worthy of his consideration. He would carefully examine each tool he picked up, as if a pitchfork or a shovel could bring some answer to the problem of suffering. He had taken to sitting down in front of Sheriff and staring at him, which made our dog uncomfortable, unused as he was to being treated as anything more than part of the furniture. He would hang his head to the side quizzically, tongue hanging out, as if waiting for an explanation. The truth was that Dad was training himself for solitude.

The men of the village seemed embarrassed. They studied the tips of their shoes. A heavy silence descended. The grass was audibly cooking beneath our feet and all around us.

Dad walked around Bagatelle, stroking her.

"She should drink something."

"In this heat."

"She's roasting alive."

"What have you given her to eat, Jean?"

"She's constipated – there's no manure."

"Her insides must be rotting."

"We should get out of here. Look at her belly. She's swelling. She's going to explode. I wouldn't like to be around when that happens."

"That would not be a pretty sight."

Dad paid no more attention to their words than to the flies massing on Bagatelle's coat. There was a tense atmosphere.

The three men seemed unable to leave, yet at a loss what to do with themselves. They looked over in my direction, in search of support. Rudy and I had stayed a little back. I said nothing, as befitted my junior position in the hierarchy. Finally, Dad stopped massaging Bagatelle's sides and, without bothering to turn his head, said, "This is none of your business."

"Of course it isn't our business. But still, you have to admit it's quite comical! She could become an attraction."

"I can already see the article in *La Feuille*."

"Lots of people would come, that's for sure. You could charge for admittance."

"Shut your mouths, you morons!" yelled Dad. "And get the hell out of here!"

"Whoa, now, take it easy! You shouldn't talk to us like that."

"Yeah, you can't speak to us like that!"

"For a start, this isn't even your field."

"Yeah. Your Bagatelle happens to be on my land," said Grin.

There was a long silence, while Anni slowly added fourteen centimetres to his annual cigarette consumption. During those moments, this act seemed to acquire an immense significance.

"I could ask you to move her."

"Don't you have anything to say?"

"You look exhausted, Jean."

There was another silence.

"I guess now that you have two women at home..."

"Must be a bit too much at your age..."

Dad grew perfectly still. He gazed at a point somewhere in the immense, featureless sky.

"They say it isn't quite like that, though..."

"Yeah. No need to mow the lawn anymore, right?"

"We heard your wife is eating nothing but grass..."

"A vagitarian!"

This last insult came from Grin, a large, greasy man in dungarees. He was knocked down first, then Pellaux, then Dind. They were flattened like bowling pins after a "strike". Dad seemed about to keep walking, into the distance, but then he turned, as if he had just remembered something important. Looking straight ahead, without so much as a glance down at the men on the ground, he strode confidently back towards them. I thought he was coming to take me and Rudy back up the hill to the Toyota. But when he reached Grin, who was trying painfully to get to his feet, he kneed him in the face, knocking him back down and making him yelp in pain. Dind, on all fours, grabbed at Dad's ankle as he passed, and received a powerful kick in the jaw. Pellaux had managed to stand up and was trying to run away, but Dad tripped him and sent him sprawling. No one made a further attempt to get up, knowing that anyone rising higher than a few centimetres off the ground would be pitilessly mown down by steel-tipped shoes. Dad was all-powerful. He had the strength of someone who no longer had any use for caution, someone indifferent to all things. He contemplated Bagatelle. He looked at the sky. He surveyed the crest of big maples, whose crowns of leaves were melting into the pale yellow of the horizon. He was breathing calmly. It wasn't an act. He had genuinely moved on. Anni smiled and shook his head.

"Jean! Stop this bullshit!" growled Dind finally, his blood-filled mouth gurgling like a blocked pipe. "You'll pay for this! This... you'll pay for it!" said Pellaux, trying again to get up.

I distinctly saw a red-tinged thread of saliva arc high into the air, as Dad's foot brutally returned him to below the decreed twenty centimetres.

"You're completely insane!" shouted Grin.

All three were now prostrate, like soldiers ducking machine-gun fire on a battlefield. Dad continued to take his time. I looked at Rudy. He was so delighted by this spectacle that frothy saliva was erupting from his parted lips. He was laughing inside. You could see it in his eyes, which squinted like those of a Tatar chief contemplating the infinity of the steppe. I had the feeling that this moment would never end. Dad seemed to be looking for something to hold onto. Anni smoked through another seventy centimetres.

"Okay, okay! I'm sorry, Jean. I shouldn't have said it..." stammered Grin.

This was his way of making it clear that he still thought it, that everyone in the village thought it, and said so in Dad's absence, and that saying it just now had been a matter of mere clumsiness, nothing more than a *faux-pas*.

Dad didn't react. He just walked between the prone bodies, without looking down.

"We're sorry. It was stupid, Jean. It was stupid. We're sorry."

"That's right, that's right, Jean. We're sorry."

"We're sorry."

Dad headed towards us, and with a wave gave the order to depart. We climbed slowly back up the gentle slope, paying no attention to what was happening behind us. We were like three cowboys sauntering off to the smell of gunpowder, having meted out justice to the rabble who'd been terrorising the little frontier town for months. I was proud. I only wondered why Dad seemed to be unaware of my existence. Yet I knew that it was no time for words. Words would have forever spoiled that shared moment of virile grace.

An ominous silence greeted us at the hen-house, and we sensed straight away that something was wrong. As we drew near, the metal walls sent out waves of heat, as if trying to drive us away. We realised that the fans had broken down; only one was still working. Through the windows, we saw that the toll of corpses, crumpled like empty bladders, was far higher than on previous days. The living hens were mute. Their beaks open, they looked as if they were panting.

"They sweat through their mouths because they can't sweat under their feathers," muttered Dad. He rubbed the back of his neck. "Go inside and pick up the dead ones."

It was an order, and we carried it out. For the sake of efficiency, Rudy held the sack while I used the tongs to collect the strangely light corpses. The survivors, watching us with their little tongues poking out, seemed to be beseeching us to put them in the bag too, as though any fate would be better than to remain trapped in this hellish furnace.

When we were done, we piled up our harvest outside, but Dad and the car were no longer there. Rudy began to sway from one foot to the other, looking around in all directions.

"Calm down, Rudy!" I said. "Calm down. Everything will be fine."

But I too was close to panic, with a hollow in the pit of my stomach and the corpse-filled sacks at my feet.

A metallic noise on the other side of the hen-house drew our attention. We walked around the building, following the tracks of the Toyota, just visible in the dead grass. It was parked against the wall, and Dad, standing on the bonnet, was busy loosening wide panels of the roof.

"What are you doing?"

Since Dad no longer paid attention to anyone, I wasn't really expecting a reply, and I didn't get one. He went on with his task. A metre-square panel fell to the ground, then another. He drove the

Toyota forward, and using the open door as a step, hoisted himself onto the hen-house roof. There, he set about removing the other panels that covered the overheated building. Unable to make an immediate repair, he had to deal first with the basic necessities, and get some air to the surviving hens as quickly as possible.

By the time we climbed back into the car, our expressions were concealed beneath masks of sweat and dust.

* * *

As soon as we arrived home, we knew that Cécile was gone. Her Renault 5 was no longer in the yard, and her laundry, which had been drying with ours on the big clothes-line near the vegetable garden, had also disappeared. Mum was busy in the kitchen. Everything was ready for us on the table: bottles of beer and lemonade, bread and cheese. Her face, pinker now that her breathing was better, was smooth and relaxed.

She didn't answer my greeting right away, but before she left the room, when we were all sitting down, she brushed by my chair and stroked my head, running her hands through my hair. I turned around to catch her eye, but she was gone already, and I only had time to see her narrow back disappearing into the doorway. Dad, who had ignored her, began to eat. Head sunk into his shoulders, he leaned over his plate as if he had to defend it against a pack of ravenous hyenas. Rudy's face was lit up by a wide smile. The knowing looks he gave to empty space, or perhaps to an audience that he alone saw, expressed his joy at being rid of this undesirable woman. Probably he imagined that, with Cécile gone, everything would go back to how it was before.

Over the next few days, perhaps it really did seem that way. He resumed his usual sequence of chores with Dad, coming and going within the narrow, immutable boundaries of his existence, with the beatific look of a Buddha on the brink of nirvana, after weeks of meditation. The pair would spend their days on the farm, returning home only when night began to darken the sky, drawing over our heads its immense, warm, grey hood.

The army was crawling over the countryside as if war had broken out. Sometimes they would come through our village in a whirlwind, raising clouds of dust. Anxious about the corn, which was dying underfoot, Dad kept watch for the arrival of the water truck. He would need the harvest to feed the next batch of chicks: buying in grain, even cheap foreign stuff, was not profitable. We were on the list for the truck to visit, but, owing to some obscure hierarchy, we had been waiting for days.

Each morning, Mum would leave very early. After depositing the day's meals in a jumbled pile on the kitchen table, she would hurry off to catch the first bus that would take her away. From my window, I would watch her exit the yard and walk down the main road with small, swift steps, each foot hurrying the other along. She seemed barely to touch the ground, as if her eagerness to be somewhere else made her levitate.

* * *

I was sitting on the low garden wall with my dove, who was conscientiously practising its walking, perhaps having dimly understood that it would never fly again. It would walk along the top of the wall up to the corner, jumping over the gaps where the stones didn't meet, before returning to its starting point. I would then stroke its head, which it must have taken as encouragement, since it would immediately start off again. In the distance, I could hear the familiar, reassuring sounds of Rudy at work in the barn. Then Dad came into view, and straight away I knew something wasn't right. He was dragging his leg. His hair was stuck together; his shirt and pants were stained with blood. One blue eyelid was closed over an eye as swollen as a pigeon's egg.

"Dad! What happened to you?" I shouted. He started, not having seen me in the shadow, then continued in a more or less straight line towards the front door. I followed close behind.

"Shit! You had an accident!"

A suspicion crept into my mind, soon growing to a certainty: Grin's band had ambushed Dad, armed with the weapons of their choice. I learned much later that they had waited outside the café, on the narrow path leading up to the church. They had used the handles of their tools to inflict their revenge.

Dad sat down in the kitchen. Motionless, he looked at the void in front of him. I didn't dare do anything. He didn't seem to be completely Dad.

"Léa! Léa! Come quickly! Come downstairs!" I shouted.

My sister came in. With air of detachment that I found somewhat theatrical, she approached Dad. "Good Lord!" she said. "He's been drinking!"

"What are you talking about?"

"I'm saying he's completely drunk! He stinks of white wine."

"What should we do?"

"We can't leave him there like that. He's covered in blood. Help me undress him! We'll have to wash him."

Léa got out a basin and filled it from the sink behind us. She didn't seem to have considered the possibility that Dad might be seriously wounded, and need to see a doctor. In her eyes, it was all very clear: he had strayed from the beaten track, come to his senses, and returned home. Now it was a matter of cleaning him up, just as you would clean up after a spillage or any other domestic accident. I was impressed.

"Hello! Gus? Is anybody there? What are you waiting for?"

"Um..."

"Dad isn't in his normal state..."

My sister was trying to tell me that we needed to undress him, that it was no big deal, that it was just a matter of helping a man who needed help. When I didn't move, she set down the tub in exasperation. "At least give me a hand!"

I pushed him a little forward on his chair, while she tugged the sleeves of his shirt to extract his arms before rolling it over his head and taking it off. The whiteness of Dad's torso, covered with tiny, frizzy hairs like the hair on his head but much sparser, contrasted with a face, neck and forearms cooked by the sun. This was the father I knew, the one who did nothing but work out in the open. But now I was discovering the other one: the Dad who, naked and with his muscles at rest, looked like a sad, defeated being. Léa began rubbing him with a washcloth that she wetted from time to time in the little metal bucket, whose water turned browner and browner.

"We'll have to take his trousers off too."

"You think?"

Léa nodded impatiently. I experienced it almost as a physical sensation, this power she had over me because she was four years older. I acted half out of filial duty and half out of submission to my sister who, without waiting, took hold of one leg.

"Come on, help me loosen the other one!"

Dad didn't own many clothes. We weren't rich. Most of the time he wore blue overalls whose cloth was like that of jeans, but not as thick. In the winter, depending on the harshness of the weather, he would put on one or two sweaters under his jacket, which he then left open to allow him to move. He changed his clothes once a week, on Mondays, and despite the fields, the barn and the pigsty, he almost never got himself dirty. Rudy, on the other hand, though he benefitted from the same clothing arrangements and performed the same jobs, looked after a single day as if he had been rolling around like an exultant pig in a vast lake of mud. Dad's neatness reflected his idea of the nobility of his profession; and the dusty, manure-filled environment in which he worked seemed to treat him with the same respectful courtesy he himself extended to all things. A farmer had to be spotless. He also insisted on the house being perfectly run, on everything being carefully put away, the laundry folded in the drawers, the dishes stacked and lined up in the cupboards, as if the order inside our home helped to maintain a more general order that influenced the quality of the harvest.

"Oh no! Please no," said Lea, giving voice to the thoughts I too was thinking. We looked at Dad's underwear. It was stained with dried blood and urine. Léa seemed to go limp. Her shoulders sagged slightly, as if from a sudden, overpowering weariness. There was nothing to be done. She dropped the wet cloth she was holding.

"Dad! Dad!" she implored.

Dad grunted and shook himself. He looked slowly around him, before getting up laboriously, leaning on the edge of the chair and lifting himself up as if his own body were a dead weight. He staggered about, like a boxer looking for the comfort of the ropes. My sister came forward, but Dad, suddenly sure of himself, stood with his legs spread wide, waving the back of his arm as if chasing away an over-insistent insect. He refused all help, defending his own private perimeter. After converting his dirty shirt and jacket into a sort of toga – one that conferred precious little dignity – he climbed the stairs slowly, puffing at each step. We followed him at a safe distance, staying to listen by his closed bedroom door. The springs of his mattress squeaked, then his laboured breathing became regular.

"He'll sleep it off," concluded my sister.

It was all too much. I felt like someone ordered to walk, but who has no idea where to put his feet. Seeing my bewildered expression, Léa smiled at me. I almost wanted her to give me a hug. Physically, my sister was like a larger, more fully realised version of Mum. It was as if, when Nature was drafting her body's secret plans, it had mixed in a few of Dad's genes to perfect its earlier creation. As for me, I was a lower-specification model of my father. I had inherited his silhouette, his hair, and a general resemblance noticed by everyone, but I lacked his defining strength, remaining small and slender for my age, as if my portion of Mum's genes were keeping me from attaining the stature of a man.

My biggest problem was that I couldn't believe that the world formed a meaningful whole. Things weren't like that. They were unique, separate from each other, like notes on a musical score. They might sometimes clash, move apart, join together to create something new, but the particles that made up reality were in their essence autonomous and unconnected. Perhaps this sense of incoherence explains why I used to dream of a hero's life.

Léa gave a slight wink, whose significance eluded me. She came close, and I breathed in the odour of her body.

"Doesn't Mum love us anymore?" I asked.

"No. She's in love. Love is a thing you can't do anything about. You become someone else."

"Is she going away to live with Cécile?"

"She isn't allergic to hay, or chicken droppings, or cat hair, as we always thought. It's just that she can't breathe the air here any longer."

"So...?"

"So when she's free to be herself, it will be different."

My sister sighed deeply several times, then informed me that these sighs were the true expression of her innermost being. "You know, Gus," she said, "I'd like to stay being me, only a much better version!"

Then she locked herself in her bedroom, which was full of objects she'd brought back in the saddlebags of her moped from distant shops that were stocked with the goods of even more distant countries: little wooden or brass boxes, colourful chiffon dolls, copper bells and sculpted elephants on plinths, trays with dried flowers scattered in their corners, and flasks of precious perfumes.

The next day, an unfamiliar smell floated through the hallway; a clinging, hospital odour. My dove was as disturbed by it as I was. Its muscles tensed up and its waist shrank to half its usual size. Its anguished cooing suddenly became very shrill. I cupped my hands around it, to try to calm it down. Mum wasn't in the kitchen, and Rudy was eating alone at the table. He seemed surprised to see me. His eyes, stretched wide open, and his open mouth, displaying a mass of *rösti*, made me think he was having difficulty remembering who I was. Finally, he smiled, breaking up the clump of potato paste between his teeth. His dilated pupils gave him the look of a dog recognising its master again, many months after being abandoned.

I took a plate and a bowl from the cupboard, and served myself from the pan on the stove. Everything had been carefully put away, except what we needed for breakfast. Nothing was out of place. The room had been swept clean, and was pervaded by the same, persistent odour of disinfectant I had detected in the hallway. It seemed more spacious than usual. The tiles shone, the table had been rubbed with polish, and the window glass had been washed with soap. The sallow morning light seemed to separate things from each other, making them unfamiliar and almost unrecognisable.

"It looks like Mum has done some housework," I said.

I could see that Rudy was lost. In his belly was the panicked fear of an animal suddenly torn from its natural habitat. He didn't say anything. I sat down, and, since we were alone, released my dove. It calmly walked towards Rudy's plate, attracted by the morsels of *rösti* lying all around it. Rudy had got up, as he did every morning, to change the straw and do the milking, but Dad hadn't come to join him. The work wasn't done, but he had come in to take his first meal at the usual time.

"Dad's still resting," I said.

Rudy shook his head. That Dad should still be in bed when it had been light for so long was beyond the sphere of his understanding.

"He's in his room," I said.

Rudy shook his head. Why stay in your bedroom if not to sleep? He looked around him, then at his empty plate, then out of the window at Sheriff, who as usual was rambling along the shadow of the house in pursuit of olfactory trails.

"Has he left?"

"No! No. Rudy, he hasn't left. He's upstairs. He's resting."

"... resting?"

What could he be resting from? Dad was never tired. He was animated by a constant energy all day long: from dawn, when he emerged, already dressed, from his bedroom, until the evening, when he went back upstairs at around ten o'clock.

"Yes. He's resting quietly, Rudy. He's upstairs."

"Is he ill?"

Rudy's face darkened. The idea had only just crossed his mind, but it had struck him with oracular force.

"No, Rudy, he's not ill."

He shook his head. Illness was the only explanation. Rudy hadn't been ill often, but the rare times it had happened – fever, sweats, trouble breathing – he had seemed to suffer more than anyone else.

"He... he's not ill," I said, but falteringly, since in the end I wasn't sure he wasn't.

My confusion served to confirm Rudy's worst fears. Just then we heard steps on the stairway. Perceiving the sudden cessation of movement around it, my dove froze, with its little beak in the air. The steps came closer, *click-click, click-click*, hard soles striking rhythmically against the stone, again and again, each one louder and clearer, until they stopped in front of the closed door of the kitchen. A few seconds went by. The door didn't open. The steps moved away, at a quicker pace.

"Mum. It's Mum!" I shouted at Rudy, before rushing into the hallway to try and catch up with her.

She was already in the middle of the yard when I called out to her with all my might. She was frightened. She was holding a suitcase that made her lean to one side, almost topple, overbalanced by a weight too great for her small arm. She didn't turn around right away. She just slowed to a halt, as though reluctantly. She was wearing the straight, blue dress she always wore. It was then that I noticed Cécile, next to her car on the other side of the road, waving to me. Or was she waving to Mum? Was it a warning? A summons? An angry gesture? Mum put down her suitcase before slowly turning around. Her face was blurred. It looked almost as if she had been beaten.

"Gus!"

" ..."

She came towards me. I noticed that she was made up, her eyelids shaded slightly with blue, her eyebrows darkened for emphasis, her lips pink and shiny, as if for a big occasion.

"Auguste!"

"..."

It was a long time since she had called me Auguste. Over the years, the name had come to seem too stately and formal for daily use. I remained silent. I wanted to look harsh. She was running away and that made her guilty. She would only regret it. So much the better if she realised that straight away...

"You... Auguste."

She walked towards me to take me in her arms. I stepped back quickly. For a brief moment, she stayed suspended on one foot, before regaining her balance.

"Gus?"

She no longer knew who she was talking to. Auguste, who had been her baby? Or Gus, the boy who had earned this nickname with his independence? I think it was her confusion that made me smile then: a small, tight grimace which I imagined was cruelly superior. I felt that I had taken the right tack.

"I have to do this, Gus! Gus... your father..."

I remained impassive. I didn't want to hear anything, especially not anything about her and Dad. Mum's face moved rapidly through one expression after another, before the tears welled up.

"Gus! I'm leaving. I'm leaving, but..."

She came forward to hug me. I couldn't entirely avoid her, but then I broke away, and shouted, "Leave me alone!"

She looked at me, incredulous. She contemplated the ochre sky, like clay above our heads. She stiffened, then she walked backwards like a robot, without taking her eyes off me. She bent her knees, grasped the handle of her suitcase, and gave me a sad smile that had almost the same value as a kiss. Mum, who was an only daughter. Mum, whose father had died four months before she was born. Mum, whose mother had never managed to get over that death, and had never tired of listing everything she lacked in order to be happy. Mum, whose mother had died a few years later from an advanced form of Paget's disease. Mum, who had been half-heartedly studying at business school when she'd met Dad. Mum, who had followed this man because she was yearning for change and loved the company of dogs, cats, all animals...

Finally turning her back to me, Mum walked calmly towards Cécile, who had already opened the car boot.

I was satisfied with myself, as I listened to the rumble of the engine fade away and disappear into the dead countryside. I felt bigger, weightier, as if something hard had expanded inside me and given me courage. My feet even seemed to make more noise than usual when they hit the ground.

I had become a man. The final image of me Mum had carried away with her was not that of her child. Very soon, little Gus would grow up and everyone would have to take him – me – seriously. From now on, I would strive to be nothing but my soul. Nothing but my pure soul, rid of all useless appendages. A powerful, polished soul, without rough bits, reduced to the essential.

* * *

A long, dismal moan, broken by an occasional shout of terror, woke me in the middle of the night. At first I thought a fox had wandered into the barn in search of mice, which happened often enough. But this noise didn't stop. I got up and went downstairs. As I crossed the yard, I almost trampled on one of our hens. A clutch had wandered astray under the bloated moon, ruffled by the warm breeze coming down from the Jura. Rudy hadn't locked them up. Now, out for a stroll together as if foxes had never existed, they were taking advantage of their unprecedented freedom. On the ground, even the tiniest fragments of seeds were brilliantly illuminated by the metallic rays of the dead planet. The hens had lost all their common sense, not their greatest asset at the best of times. Sheriff was watching over them anxiously, trying to keep them together, dashing to and fro like a sheep dog around his flock. I sensed the bewilderment in his gaze when I stroked the top of his head as I went by. A wind of madness was blowing over our heads; a feeling of dread was in all of us.

In the barn, dimly lit by three bare lightbulbs, Rudy stood motionless, arms hanging at his sides, petrified with fear in the midst of the cows. They were pulling at their tethers, stomping violently on the floor and mooing for help. I came closer to his face, which was gleaming with sweat.

"What's going on, Rudy?"

He was somewhere else, a far-off place to which I had no access. I grabbed his arm and squeezed it, calling out his name again and again, before his mind re-entered his body.

"I don't know," he said.

The hay hadn't been changed for several days, and gave off a powerful ammoniac stench. The cows were knee-deep in a seething mass of bacteria that was beginning to inflame their teats. I noticed their swollen udders, the veins bulging.

"Haven't you mucked them out? Or milked them?"

"No."

For someone used to everything always being the same, who never had to make a single decision, the events of the last few days had been a cosmic upheaval equivalent to the disappearance of the dawn. The automatic movements of Rudy's daily labours were linked by invisible threads to my father, always by his side. In the absence of external forces, he was paralysed. He no longer knew what to do.

"It's okay! Calm down, Rudy!"

"They're going to explode!"

"No, they're not."

The animals were stamping their hooves, upset by our presence. It was as if they believed we had come to transport them to the slaughterhouse. Its eyes rolling upwards, one cow twisted to catch hold of her own teat with her mouth, freeing herself of her pain by sucking like a calf. Rudy began to sweat in big drops. Nothing was normal.

"It's okay, Rudy, it's okay."

"They're going to explode!"

"No, they're not, Rudy! They'll dry off."

"It's a catastrophe!"

"They've stopped making milk," I said, seeing that he hadn't understood what was meant by "dry off". It was too late. The prospect of our animals literally desiccating had plunged him into a bottomless abyss of terror.

I tried again. "They're full. We'll milk them. Then everything will go back to the way it was before."

"... was before."

We started milking. Rudy worked next to me, his jaws clenched in disapproval because I was much slower and clumsier than Dad. He didn't take me seriously as a boss. His opinion of me fell even lower when he realised that I had no idea what to do with the filled buckets. The dairy wasn't open yet, and in any case I wasn't allowed to drive the tractor on the main road. The milk would heat up and slowly spoil in the aluminium containers. Rudy's cheeks were shining like two polished apples. He was lost, more lost than anyone in the world. His mind, with nothing familiar to cling to, had simply abandoned him, left him alone, like a shipwrecked man drifting on a raft tossed by the inscrutable ocean. His head down, he looked compulsively in all directions, from time to time raising his eyes as if he was trying to work out where the next almighty blow would come from. I took his hand. His palm was soft and his fingers limp.

"Rudy! Rudy! Calm down. Calm down. Everything's fine. Everything's fine," I murmured, drawing out the vowels.

He looked right, then left, then at the cows, who had rediscovered their natural placidity; then again right, left, and back at the cows, who were still placid. This seemed to surprise him. Finally, he stared at me with his small, wet, drowned-man eyes. I couldn't leave him alone. I went to fetch my mattress and dove.

Rudy began to make a careful inventory of all the objects in his room, located between the pigsty and a narrow corridor that led through the farm buildings. He moved each item a few millimetres in one direction, before returning it exactly to its original position. He checked the configuration of all the drawings he'd pinned up, which covered an entire wall. I regularly presented him with new pictures, and they had come to form a collage of everything that made up his daily environment. Then, he verified the precise coordinates of each one of the treasures that were lined up on his shelf: the flask of vetiver, the china dogs that Mum gave him for each birthday. Gradually, this ritual calmed him down, confirming each thing in its immutable place. At last, he undressed, rearranging his clothes several times on the back of his chair before getting into bed. We wished each other good night at regular intervals, until we decided that we'd hit on just the right intonation. Plunging his head into his pillow, Rudy threw himself into the task of sleeping, as if this wasn't something that took care of itself, but required serious commitment. With the zeal of a wise man who has come to view slumber as the highest form of human activity, he began to snore.

Stretching out on an old mattress I had placed at the foot of his bed, I opened my cartoon book. Immediately, I became Time's master, free to race through the whole strip, or else to linger over each frame to savour a multitude of exquisite details. After a first swift reading, greedily turning the pages to see what would happen, I would go back at my leisure, re-reading certain passages several times, pausing over a vignette, entering the book as you would enter a room in a museum. I drifted lazily around the landscape sketched in the background: the trees, the purple-roofed village, the strands of mist in the distance, the carefully positioned flowers and butterflies, the grassy molehills in the foreground, and the little animals – they all hummed together in a harmonious ensemble.

I set myself down at a street corner. There was a square, some pigeons, two lovers on a bench, a few scraps of litter floating in the wind, a single patch of grass protected by parapets and pruned hedges, and a bronze sculpture turned green with age, its head and shoulders covered with bird droppings. Here was a reality where everything was motionless, separated from before and separated from after. I would have liked to live in a drawing the whole time.

VII

The army finally showed up at our farm.

I saw the Jeep roar into our yard at top speed. I saw our hens, who were becoming ever more arrogant in the sun, decide collectively that there was no point taking evasive action. I saw the Jeep plough through them, then stop abruptly and reverse in a cloud of feathers, leaving three bloody victims horribly squashed on the stones. Two soldiers jumped out to assess the damage, whereupon Sheriff, who must have been dozing in some shady corner, deemed it necessary to rush at them, barking madly. When he saw the little corpses, he first veered towards them, then stopped in his tracks. His barking turned into yapping, then into strange, sounds, like the creaking of a rusty door hinge, that seemed as if they couldn't have come from a living creature. Finally, he fell silent, and flattened himself against the ground. The two soldiers, berets in hand, scanned the surroundings for another living soul. I decided to emerge from the shadow of our big elm.

After weeks of combat against a relentless enemy, the men had a defeated look. Their bodies, marinated in sweat, had expanded within their uncomfortably tight uniforms. One of them, poking a finger into the dirty collar of an outfit too thick for any summer, let alone this one, fixed his gaze on the dove on my shoulder. "I don't get it," he said. "Are your hens suicidal or what?"

Not having considered this possibility, I was at a loss how to answer. Besides, he seemed to be expecting a response from my bird as much as from me.

"Usually they keep away from cars, don't they? We're sorry. Still, we'll fill out a form and you'll be recompensed."

"..."

"The pigeon..."

"It's a dove."

"The dove, then – is it tame?"

"Yes."

They were looking for Dad. I told them he wasn't around. They asked where my mother was. I said she wasn't around either. They asked me where they could find one or the other. They were growing insistent, so I said my father was very ill, and I didn't know where my mother was. This information upset them. The truck was on site and ready for action, but they needed someone to help with the task – and to sign the government forms. At this point, the one who seemed to be the leader said, "It looks like your dog is dead."

"Watering can!" I shouted.

The two soldiers recoiled towards their vehicle as Rudy arrived at a run, holding the overflowing can high in front of him at arm's length. Open-mouthed, they watched as he distributed water from the spout in careful, precise streams, starting with the tips of the dog's paws and ending with his nose. With his stuck-out tongue pointing the way, Rudy applied himself with supernatural concentration, as if the efficacy of the cure depended upon his leaving no single part of Sheriff dry.

"It's just the heat," I explained.

"No. It was when he saw the squashed chickens. Your dog is too emotional."

"… too emotional," Rudy repeated.

"That's possible," I agreed.

"Yup. It's not just the heat. It's the emotion that made him faint," said the other soldier.

"The emotion that made him faint," echoed Rudy, as he attempted to absorb this new idea. I knew that from now on he would repeat this intriguing phrase whenever our dog's name was mentioned.

Sheriff got up and calmly shook himself. He was a creature of habit, and passing out in the heat before waking up under a cool shower had become part of his normal routine. I even suspected him of feigning his fits in order to receive the benefit of our attentive and refreshing care.

The soldiers eventually agreed that I could come with them. They needed to make sure they watered the right field, and in the end, nobody gave a crap about the paperwork.

I climbed into the back of the Jeep, and we drove across the land towards the theatre of operations. They were carrying rifles, which clashed with every jolt, making a noise like clanging saucepans. Perhaps, in this desert-like terrain, they thought they might actually have to use their weapons to defend their precious cargo of water.

The water truck and three more soldiers were waiting for us in the middle of the road. I greeted the leader, a tall, moustachioed man with very white skin. Instead of a beret, he had a cap on his head, and he seemed to be suffering much less from the surrounding heat than his men. His cold hand was that of an animal capable of adapting its temperature to its circumstances. He showed me a rough map, on which our holdings were highlighted, then pointed to our stretch of corn. I confirmed that our land did indeed correspond to what was marked on his map. He gave the order, and after a delay of a minute or two, the men got to work, unfurling the hose and turning on the pump, which began to hum.

The truck moved slowly over our field, as two soldiers in the back operated the hose. The first plants collapsed as soon as the powerful jet of water struck them. A few cobs of corn were flung skywards, narrowly missing our heads as they fell back to earth. The men adjusted their aim, spraying at a point above the target, so that a dense rain poured down on the crop, which crackled like wood in the fireplace. When they had finished, I signed in place of my father at the bottom of the paper the officer held out to me. The soldiers left in a hurry, returning to the lake in order to refill their tank for other urgent irrigations.

The field was in ruins. The water had done nothing but slide in little streams over the black earth, as hard as a reptile's skin. It had accumulated in dirty, dust-covered puddles in the hollows, from where it would evaporate without ever penetrating the earth to work its magic. The long stems of the plants were still crackling. It sounded as if a fire were slowly consuming them from inside. The desiccated leaves and the beard around the corn husks looked like oakum on the verge of spontaneously combusting. The ground was strewn with little white fish, some of them still flapping their tails. They had been sucked from their habitat, to be tossed about in an immense, dark aquarium, before ending their lives with their bellies in the air, floundering in despair on the bare earth.

* * *

I met Maddie on Queen Berthe's way, just past the Susten, the highest point in the commune. There was a sort of monument there, made of a few stones, which commemorated the major land redistribution that had taken place from 1941 to 1943. As war raged through the rest of the world, and armies carved out vast new empires over heaps of corpses, our villagers had peacefully negotiated various land exchanges to improve their lot and aid their work in the fields. In the centre of this modest, sepulchre-like edifice stood our Tree of Liberty, planted in 1903 to mark the centenary of our independence from French occupation. I was walking under the tree's hot and not very refreshing shade, when Maddie appeared from behind a thicket, where, she told me without embarrassment, she had been relieving an urgent need.

"Everything's dead."

"What?"

"I said everything's dead."

"Yeah."

"It seems like nothing is held together anymore. The hedge isn't connected to the meadow. The road doesn't go with the sky. That tree over there – it looks like it's floating. There's too much distance between things, don't you think?"

I'd have preferred to walk along this white path by myself. I was finding Maddie's closeness very unpleasant. She couldn't resist cleaving to me, so that her thigh brushed my leg at every step, and her shoulder rubbed against mine. She was looking up at me with her big blue eyes, which always gave me the sense of an unfinished soul. They were the vacant eyes of a calf discovering a world it cannot understand.

She talked to me about crawling insects that had roasted in the depths of their holes as in an oven; about flying insects that had fallen from the air like withered fruit, exhausted from beating their wings through a furnace; about all the little mammals

– shrews and field mice, hedgehogs and weasels – that had died of thirst. According to her, these modest, almost-invisible life-forms were what stopped the whole of nature from unravelling and splitting apart. Their disappearance was a bad omen. Even the butterflies had departed for far-off places where flowers still grew.

"Did they water your field?"

"Yeah."

"My father says it's too late."

"Hmm..."

"My father says the roots are already burnt from below."

I felt like asking her which father she meant. The father who had conceived her then abandoned her? Or the father who had taken her in but cared about her no more than the mangy cats with worm-filled ears who squatted in his barn? But my malicious thoughts failed to blossom into speech, and I only said, "You're getting on my nerves!"

She gazed at me with a mixture of surprise and irritating tenderness. We stopped at a grey bush with no shade.

"What's the matter, Gus?"

"I told you. You're getting on my nerves."

"It's because of that woman. The one we saw at the river."

"Shut up!"

"My father says your mum has left."

"She hasn't left."

"Oh really?"

"She... she went on holiday. For a few days."

"On holiday?"

"Yeah. She's coming back."

Her stupid, shapeless face creased into a disbelieving smirk. No one in the village ever went on holiday! She nodded. I felt sure that she pitied me.

"Your bird looks sad," she said, pressing herself against me. I felt the firmness of her breasts against my chest. "It looks like he's shrunk. His tail is all shrivelled up."

She wanted to stroke the dove. I tried to cover it and our hands touched. It took me a moment to realise that, having failed to reach my bird, she was attempting to entwine her fingers around mine. It seemed like a gesture of tenderness. I shoved her violently, extending my arms fully to get her as far away as possible. She fell backwards, into what remained of the grass at the side of the path.

Alarmed, my dove had jumped off my shoulder. After a pathetic attempt at flight, it lay in a ball about a metre from Maddie, who was flat on her back. I looked at Maddie, motionless on the ground, her legs spread, her skirt hitched up to mid-thigh; I looked at her underwear between her legs, the same colour as my bird. I went over to her. Her eyes were closed, but she wasn't unconscious. She was breathing normally, gently, as though she were having a mid-afternoon snooze. She was deliberately keeping her eyelids shut so as not to see me. I kicked her lightly in the hip to wake her up. She didn't react. I began to kick harder, then harder still, until I was kicking her inert body with all my strength. "Dirty little wicked beast!" I said. My head and all my thoughts were filled with anger – a wholesome, satisfying anger that diffused though my body something sweet and calming. Maddie no longer existed. Mum no longer existed. I no longer existed. I could have killed her and simply gone on my way, without turning back, because we were no one anymore.

"Stop! Stop!"

I saw my dove in a ball, a few feet away in the grass, saw Maddie's mouth between her dirt-covered arms, raised to try and protect her face. One of her legs seemed strangely bent, its knee at an odd angle. I kicked again and again and again, harder and harder.

"I'm hurt! Stop, Gus. Please stop!"

"What?"

"I'm hurt," whispered Maddie.

I began to strike her more softly. I looked around, at the grey hedge slowly turning to charcoal in the sun; at the airless, cloudless sky without a single bird or insect flying through it; at the path, sharply outlined in the nearby dark fields, but hazy and blurred at the horizon; at the black line of distant mountains that framed us.

Maddie's eyes were full of tears, but you wouldn't say that she was crying. It was more like a tensing of all the muscles in her face.

"I'm hurt."

An immense, dizzying distance still separated us.

"What's the matter, Gus? You're crazy!"

She struggled to her feet, and made a preliminary inspection of her body, massaging herself gently to check that the various layers of her being were still in place. She passed her hands over her face, as if she wanted to erase it. I wasn't sorry. How could such an act, without any motive or reason, be wrong? Maddie looked at me, without hostility. She took a few limping steps. One of her legs buckled under her weight, as if it might collapse at any moment. I watched her recover, little by little, as she walked around me. She was like a wounded animal. Her body had betrayed her, but she had not lost the desire to function normally. I thought of my dove, hopping about with its neck outstretched, straining to take off.

"Good! I'm not too hurt," she said finally, with scientific detachment, after several trips back and forth.

It was as if we had played a game, and she had lost; as if she were used to losing, and games always went wrong for her.

"What should we do now?" She came up to me, and pressed against my stomach. "We're quite near the reservoir."

"Yeah."

"I know how to get into it."

"So?"

"The water's clear. And ice-cold... Come on! I'll show you."

The village had had its own pumping station since the end of the war. At that time, after the famers had heroically and single-handedly fed the nation for the past six years, it was anticipated that everyone would want to live near fields. As a result, the rural population would naturally increase and villages like ours would prosper. Our ambitious pumping station, built under such post-war expectations, was eight metres deep. Tapping into the secret, subterranean streams that flowed into the surface river, it had a theoretical capacity of several thousand cubic metres per hour, and fed every pipe, hose and tap in the village. To this day, it stands at the edge of the forest, like a real house in miniature, with a pointy roof, a door and a window.

I took Maddie's arm. She was having trouble walking straight. As she leaned against me, I smelled her hair in my nostrils: dried grass mixed with old apples, burnt earth and sweat. She had been spying on the station attendant, and now, after taking five long strides, then seven, then five more, each time changing direction at right angles like a pirate returning to a desert island to recover buried treasure, she found the key, hidden under a stone.

We entered a tiny room with four walls covered in white tiles. Opposite us was a large electronic console bristling with pointers, dials, and red and green indicators. I was starting to feel a little disappointed, when Maddie pointed gleefully at a round trap-door at our feet. I could hear the sound of drips far below, each one with its own musical identity. We had found it. The passage that led to the water buried in the depths of the earth. Maddie opened the trap-door. I put my dove down. Evidently not fired by any intrepid desire to explore the underworld, it made itself into a placid little ball on the top of the control panel.

It was a damp, black hole with a very narrow ladder, whose rungs plunged into the darkness. Maddie pointed out that you could sense the watery presence at the bottom, because there was a coolness that rose up, like smoke out of a chimney. She took a little torch hanging from a nail, and slipped it into my mouth. We'd need light, she said. She was very excited. I couldn't speak. The beam from my lips illuminated her freckled face.

Her excitement made up my mind. We took off our shoes. I entered the narrow tunnel first, my back against the sticky wall. It had been wet for so many years that I was afraid it had been eaten away by invisible mould, and that my contact with it might make the stone instantly crumble, hurling us both to the bottom in a huge din of rubble. The rungs grew more and more slippery. When I looked up for reassurance, my beam illuminated Maddie as she descended fearlessly just above me. The angle and lighting were somewhat unusual. With each step, her buttocks parted a little, and a hollow formed under her white panties, which, aided by Maddie's twisting movements, rolled up until they were nothing more than a thin strand of cloth with the sole function of highlighting the two luminous spheres on either side. It was no longer Maddie. It was a part of Maddie. A part that could make me change my view of Maddie as a whole.

"Wuhuh…" The flashlight between my teeth made consonants impossible. I stopped. I couldn't see Maddie's face, only the curves and creases of her looming rear end.

"What did you say?"

"Wuhuh!"

"...?"

"WUH-UH!"

"We're there?"

"Uh-huh..."

"Keep going! It's not very deep."

I dipped a foot into the freezing water, and let myself fall.

"Is it cold?"

"Yeah."

I was in up to my stomach. My trousers stuck to my legs like a second, ill-fitting skin. I took off my shirt and draped it from the ladder. Illuminated by the circle of light emanating from my mouth, Maddie took off her T-shirt, which she carefully rolled around a rung, then slipped off her skirt, lifting each foot in turn, and put it in the same place. She removed her underwear, hung it next to the rest of her clothes, and leapt in beside me. The vaulted ceiling was sweating. Drops fell all around us: *drip-drip, plock-plock.*

"Do you think there are any animals in here, like salamanders?" she asked.

She launched herself forward to swim. The water in the little underground lake came to life. The waves created by her breaststroke bounced off the walls, and merged to form other, larger ones. Maddie gradually came closer and closer, calm in the midst of the stormy waters, staring at me whenever she crossed my beam of light. She was incredibly naked under her gleaming liquid robes. Never had I seen her so tall, so long, so well-made. The cold water had cured her of all earthly pains. She began to brush gently against me, as if she wanted to wind herself around me.

"Come on..." she pleaded.

I mimed to her that the flashlight had to stay dry. She leaned over, took it from my mouth, and put it in hers. Dazzled, I closed my eyes. Maddie put her cheek against my shoulder; when she caressed me, I pressed my lips against her wet hair. We were very far from the other human beings struggling and sweating on the surface, and when her hand went lower and opened my trousers, when she rubbed her crotch against my thigh with an uneven, whistling breath, I had the strange, slightly terrifying feeling that we had left the world above our heads behind us forever. I leaned over towards a breast made stiff by the cold, and straight away it filled my mouth. The beam of light came and went on the wall like a distress signal. I squeezed her hard, too hard, without understanding why it didn't hurt her, without understanding how she could continue moving, why she wasn't suffocated by my embrace.

We hadn't noticed that the water level had perceptibly lowered. The pumps had begun to throb. We stayed still for a long while, clinging to each other amidst the gurgling and bubbles, prisoners in the belly of the earth, which now seemed to want to digest us. Maddie slowly detached herself from me, with a serious look. Neither of us was the emotional type. All she said was: "You do realise, Gus, now your sperm will come out of all the taps in the village!"

* * *

The sky had changed. We couldn't see the sun anymore. It had finally merged with the atmosphere, which was dark yellow, saturated with microscopic particles, and as dense as caramel.

Maddie, having carefully locked the station and returned the key, looked up. "What's happening? The air has gone all hard." She passed her hand back and forth in front of her face, as if to push away a viscous fluid.

"Everything's electric."

"Maybe it's the end of the world."

"The sky's looks like it's going to burst."

It was at that precise instant that the first drops crashed onto the ground, with the violence of missiles hitting their targets: one, then three, then ten, then countless more, raising the dust all around us. The rain had picked up the dirt that had been suspended in the air for months, and painted long, black lines on our faces. At the first rumbles of thunder – impossible to tell whether they came from above or below – followed immediately by flashes of lightning that for a split second transformed reality into a white screen, I began to run towards the village. I was vaguely aware that Maddie was behind me. We were both running through curtains of water so solid they seemed to contain iron filings.

As we passed the round field, I paused, and tried to spot Bagatelle below. I thought I could make out her impassive silhouette under the deluge, but the next instant a gust of wind heavy with beating rain made everything darker. The huge maples made terrible cracking noises. I thought of my grandfather, perhaps still in the woods near his horse. My mouth full of water and dust, I saw the vague outline of Maddie, still running, disappear around a bend. Everything was a strange, greenish tint, until there was a sharp crack and for a fraction of a second everything was very bright and clear. Then the rain redoubled in intensity. I had to find a shelter as quickly as possible. I began running again, my dove balled up under my T-shirt. My feet were floating in their inundated shoes, and I had the feeling that I was no longer on firm ground, that I was lost in an in-between world.

Arriving at our yard, I almost ran into the Toyota. Rudy was standing on one side, Dad on the other. They didn't move when they saw me, as if they had been immobilised by the water that drummed down on their heads.

"Where have you been?" shouted Dad.

I wasn't sure if it was a real question. Dad was the only person who from time to time concerned himself with my whereabouts, but he had been in his room for days without taking an interest in anything. Also, it was hardly the ideal time or place to discuss the matter, so when he held open the door of the Toyota, I slid wordlessly onto the back seat.

At last, I had a chance to extract my dove from its cramped refuge under my soaking shirt. It looked as if it had been through a vigorous cycle in the washing machine. Not that the experience seemed to have caused it the least distress. I placed it on my shoulder. The bird's easy-going nature was beginning to really annoy me. Its indifference to the external world, even in its most unpleasant or dangerous aspect, made it seem more like an object than an animal. I was starting to understand how this creature could be a magician's accessory, no different from a deck of cards, a set of beakers, or a top hat.

We were all dripping, so that it seemed to be raining inside the car. Rudy beamed at me from the seat next to me. He had rediscovered his unconditional trust in things. The machinery of the world was once again whirring smoothly; everything was back in normal working order. He would have liked to see me share his joy at Dad taking matters firmly in hand like this. No doubt it would have done him good to give vent to the euphoria that was filling his head, to share the happiness that was overwhelming hism and overflowing from his pores. But he was not capable of making words to express these complex feelings, only the saliva that streamed from his half-open mouth. I didn't share his optimism about our future, but I stretched out my arm to squeeze his knee briefly, as a sign of empathy.

The roads leading the hen-house had been transformed into

torrents of mud. Apart from the distant lines of trees visible behind the clouds of vapour, everything seemed to have dissolved into formlessness. We drove very slowly. My father gripped the steering wheel, with the muscles in his neck and arms tensed, as if he were participating in the car's exertions, its tyres skidding this way and that, flinging up gobs of mud to mark the windows with long, brown streaks.

We pulled up a few metres from the hen-house entrance. There were gaps in the roof, where Dad had removed the panels to lower the temperature inside the building. The wind had massively widened these openings, crushing and tearing whole sheets of corrugated iron. We got out of the car. The storm had abated. A heavy but unhurried rain fell, as though, having done its duty and filled the heavens with violence at the height of the storm, it was now free to pour down at its ease. We stood for a while under the shower, looking at the decapitated hen-house. Rudy and I stayed a few feet behind Dad. We were waiting for him to make the first move. He didn't want to discover the truth too quickly, and neither did we.

When Dad pushed open the door, the water came up to his calves. Reluctantly, we entered the changing room. It was flooded with over fifty centimetres of dirty liquid. Our white jumpsuits hung absurdly and uselessly from their pegs. There was no longer any point in taking sanitary precautions. The rain was falling though the gaps in the roof. The food trays, suspended by ropes, were waterlogged, filled with a thick, stinking soup in which grains of corn, whitish traces of excrement, and corpses were floating. The livid, bloated carcasses of the hens undulated on the water, stirred by waves created by the few survivors, who, necks craned to keep their heads in the air, despairingly waved their wings like oars. Dad remained still.

His face showed no emotion. I knew this was a sign of extreme agitation, of a profound and paralysing pain that had stopped up the usual channels of feeling.

It must have seemed to Dad that a cosmic shift in the natural order had taken place during his brief absence. One world – the lower one, that you hoped to master through work, though daily care of your animals and plants, that you could almost understand because it was almost human, and part of a universe subject to our human will – this world had yielded to another, different kind of nature, lofty, distant, often incomprehensible, yet always imposing itself on us. Sometimes this higher nature would show itself by signs that Dad knew how to interpret: a shift in the wind or in the colour of the clouds. Every morning, he would stop in the hall in front of our barometer's round dial to inspect the tiniest expansion or contraction of the mercury column.

It was Mum's departure that had marked the start of the high world invading the low one. She was the cause of the sudden catastrophic rent in the membrane of the universe, and everything was very directly her fault. I wanted to throw up from the stench.

Dad suddenly remembered that he knew what to do in every situation. "We have to get the live ones out," he said.

He pushed open the glass door, and all three of us were engulfed in water up to our knees. The technique was to catch hold of the birds by their frail necks, just under their tiny heads, and pull them gently upwards, like reeds from a marsh. They were sticky. You had to be gentle, or you might squeeze out the last breath they still had. From time to time, one would slip through our hands and fall back in, sinking straight down, and we had to hurry to recover it, stirring the disgusting liquid blindly in the hope of catching hold of a claw or a wing and lifting it out of the death-trap. Dad walked about in big strides, and, without bending, seized all the chickens within his reach, carrying them in clusters of three.

Gradually, we transported them outside onto the platform in front of the entrance, where, huddled together, stunned by cold and fear, they stayed perfectly still. After one horribly close encounter with the aquatic element, they now found themselves under an immense and rain-swollen sky. They were not about to wander off into this threatening universe.

We didn't bother counting them. Of the ten thousand that Dad had hoped to sell, there must have been fewer than a hundred survivors, shivering under their wet feathers. I stood next to him under the eaves. The fine, white, stubborn rain seemed as if it would never stop, as if the clouds had won a final victory in their endless war of attrition against the drought. Dad looked at the pitiable remains of his brood. It was bankruptcy. How would he ever pay back the loan? How could he repair the ruined hen-house?

I met his gaze. He looked at me for a long time, with infinite tenderness, and I understood that he hated these wretched birds, which had wounded his honour. They were not like our cows out in the meadow or in the barn, or our well-kept pastures, or our neat fields of barley and corn. They were not our allies. They were traitors; they had become enemies.

We were standing there, soaking wet but sheltered from the rain, adrift in a kind of no man's land, when a loud bang, followed immediately by a strange crackling sound, made us jump.

"Where's Rudy?" asked Dad.

"I don't... he must have stayed inside..."

"Shit."

We rushed back into the building, noticing immediately that a further section of the metal roof had given way. A wide piece of corrugated iron floated among the dead birds. During its fall, it had ripped open the pipes carrying the feed, and torn out the electric wires, which gave off loud sprays of sparks as they came into contact with the water. Dad ran into the changing room to turn off the fuse box and cut the electricity. I was the one who discovered Rudy. He was floating on his stomach. I knelt down to turn him over and take his head out of the water.

"Rudy! Rudy!"

His eyes were open. They were full of dirty water, and covered with a dull, unreflecting veil.

My father came up behind me. "Oh my God!"

We would never know for sure whether Rudy, who must have stayed behind in the hope of saving a final hen, was killed instantaneously by the falling piece of roof, or was knocked out and then drowned, or was electrocuted, but we settled on the first version as the most bearable for all of us. We carried him into the car, as if there was still some point in sheltering him. At the time, I didn't cry.

Dad arranged him comfortably on the back seat. Gently, he replaced Rudy's lock of hair on his forehead, in a gesture that reminded me of the caress parents give their children last thing at night. Abandoning the hens, we brought Rudy back home without saying a word. I told myself it was out of respect, because he was no longer there to hear us.

* * *

The storms of the summer of 1976 beat down upon the baked earth. They shredded the crops, already exhausted after their long fight against the drought. In some places, they uprooted every last dying plant. The fields, stripped bare by waves of mud, became as smooth as pebbles. The storms carried away a part of our countryside.

The big elm in our garden, like all the elms in the country, began to die.

* * *

Léa gave a little wave when she saw us enter the concert hall. She was surrounded by young East Germans, with the festive look of convicts on leave. They gave the impression of being entirely at her service, stretching their shiny, too-tight city suits as they inclined smilingly in her direction. How could it have been any different? Léa was dazzling. All eyes were on her, and her alone. The other girls, already seated with their clarinets or violins, their faces sad or severe, seemed resigned to their fate as mere foils for her beauty.

We took two empty seats in the last row. Dad's neck looked somehow stiff, and he wore a strange expression, at times a little too focused, at times vague. The musicians began to tune their instruments, in no particular order; the sound was jarring and unpleasant.

Mum and Cécile were sitting right at the front, and realised that Dad's expression was vague when he was looking at the stage, intense when he was contemplating Mum. He couldn't stop himself moving from one to the other, though he lingered longer on Mum than on the musicians. Neither of us was in the mood to sit and listen to a symphony, but Léa had promised Rudy he could come to the concert dressed in his Sunday clothes, and he had talked to me about it many times. It was clear that he had been imagining some kind of high-society occasion; perhaps he had even dreamt of meeting the chosen one who would at last take him out of his solitude. It was for Rudy that Léa would be playing.

Bent over their instruments, the musicians began the first

movement. At a stroke, they were transformed by suffering. They grimaced, their lips squashed against the chin-rests of their violins; they sweated copiously, with furrowed brows, as they blew into their trumpets; their pinched mouths twisted as they drew the bows of their cellos. If they stopped playing for a moment, they remained nervous and dazed, awaiting the arrival of fresh torments. Léa's face, too, was marked with pain. I had never seen her so preoccupied, penetrated by something that wasn't her, and that disfigured her.

All I could see of Mum were her shoulders and her tiny head, leaning over to almost touch Cécile's. I wondered if they were discreetly holding hands as they listened to the New World Symphony. Mum had been twenty-one when I was born. Now I was thirteen and she was abandoning us. Was she twenty-one again? Had her life with us been some kind of error, a glitch, a digression outside of time? Perhaps she really was a young woman again...

The after-concert reception had been organised in honour of the musicians from the East. Dad seemed to have lost all ability to bend. He stood holding a glass of white wine, feet planted in the gravel in the shade of a plane tree. His back was straight, his suit tight around the armholes, his body seized by a stiffness that would stay with him for the rest of his life. The musicians mingled with the crowd, greeting admiring parents, moving from one group to another, excited and garrulous, as if they had all just been through a terrible ordeal and couldn't quite get over being back in the normal world.

I began to drink the wine laid out on long tables, amidst salty breadsticks and delicate canapés. My head was already spinning when Léa came over, still wearing her bewildered survivor's look. Dad reassured her that she had been wonderful, that she had played magnificently, and I echoed him word for word. She explained to us how difficult it was, after the rumpus of the horns, to leap from the exuberance of the first movement to the meditativeness of the second, expansive and sad, and we agreed, as if we understood her perfectly how hard it must have been. After a minute or two, Léa went back to her friends.

I had the strange feeling that we no longer existed, that there was a void around us, that the light was different where we were... Everyone was talking, moving from group to group with glass in hand, but nobody penetrated the magic circle that separated us from the crowd. We knew no one. We remained prudently motionless, as though we were standing in the centre of a minefield. Dad was staring at Mum and Cécile, who, side by side under the blue shade of a plane tree, were laughing with a group of young, female musicians. Mum glanced furtively in our direction and, despite the distance, the white wine, the dazzling sun, I knew she had caught Dad's eye for a fraction of a second. He was tense, as if he were making a strenuous physical effort.

"Bitch!" I muttered.

Dad turned slowly towards me. The word floated dangerously in the air between us. I heard it reverberate there, as if it hadn't come out of my mouth. Then everything shattered.

When I came to, I was on the ground. I shook my head from side to side, my eyes still closed, trying to get things back into their proper places. There was a crowd around me. A woman leaned over and gave me a handkerchief. I took it mechanically. She rubbed her chin to show me that I should wipe my own. It was only then that I felt the blood dripping from my open lip.

"What's wrong with you? Hitting a child! Are you crazy?" I heard someone say.

Dad was ignoring me. His attention had moved onto something else. And there was no Mum, leaning anxiously over me...

* * *

I didn't know how the soothsayers of Antiquity regarded white doves, but it was clear to me that the arrival of the wounded bird in our household had been an ill omen that should have put us on our guard.

That night, the acrid smell of the droppings which carpeted my room caught in my throat. I snatched from its perch the useless, unfeeling creature, so indifferent to my unhappiness, and hurled it like a grenade from the window. It spun through the air, stabilised itself long enough to unfold its wings, and fluttered pitifully over the roofs. But when it tried to turn and fly back, it suddenly lost altitude, landing violently on its back in the garden, less than a metre from the big red tomcat from the neighbouring farm. It had no time to get back on its feet. Collecting its prey in its jaws, the cat moved off calmly to find a quiet place to skin it, as if it were quite normal for his dinner to arrive in this way, by airmail.

So my stupid dove ended its stupid existence in this sad fashion. Its death was the closing act of that summer of 1976, and nothing else abnormal – that is, apart from the normally abnormal – happened at our place.

* * *

Two days after the catastrophe in the hen-house, a hearse came to pick up Rudy's body. We had put him in the living room, now transformed into a funerary chapel. In his work clothes amidst our household décor, his hands clasped over his chest, he looked ill-at-ease, as if he were making an effort to stay still, so as not to take up too much room in this unfamiliar, slightly intimidating place. Even though my parents had never forbidden him access to the different parts of the house, he knew only the hallway leading to the kitchen, and had never adventured upstairs. His real territory had been the farm buildings.

Revived by the drop in temperature, Sheriff paced frantically to and fro for days in search of fresh tracks that might take him to his vanished companion. Our life seemed to have gone down a gear. We spoke in low voices even when we were far from the living room. We made as little noise as possible, as if we all felt ashamed of being alive in the house where this dead man lay. Perhaps we were also trying not to attract further unwanted attention from the powerful gods who watched over us, and who had made their displeasure at recent events all too clear.

Dad spent a long time standing in the yard, doing nothing but gazing at the horizon. He gave no sign of noticing when my grandfather's silhouette tottered into view. When Anni finally tapped him on the shoulder, Dad turned towards him slowly, after a few seconds of delay, as if a very complex series of manoeuvres were needed to effect this quarter-rotation. Anni rummaged through the bulging pocket of his jacket, in search of his pack of cigarettes. It took him a long time to fish them out, since just at that moment a powerful coughing fit took hold of him, shaking him from head to foot. Dad didn't bat an eyelid as his father eructed, spat and heaved, seemingly about to break into pieces.

Anni had been with Bagatelle when the storm broke. At first, he had taken shelter in his thicket, but round drops the size of grapes pierced the anaemic foliage of the maples, and he had made for the village, where Rose, the old cousin who looked after him, had been waiting anxiously. She had dried him from head to foot, but it was no good. His emaciated body had absorbed a fatal excess of wetness, which had penetrated his very bones, and could no longer be got rid of. Three months later, it would kill him with what the doctor, for lack of a better term, diagnosed as pneumonia.

Anni finally got his dreadful shaking under sufficient control to bring the little flame of his match into contact with the tip of his fourteen centimetres of cigarette. The smoke entered and exited through his nostrils, filled his lungs with dry air, and calmed him down. He held the pack out to Dad, who took one, leaning towards him to light it. It was the first time I had seen him smoke. They stood side by side without saying anything, gazing into the void, enveloped by a grey cloud. Dad looked even stiffer and larger than usual.

Anni wanted to go upstairs to see Rudy. As he passed in front of me, he gave me a few taps on the shoulder, similar to the ones he gave Bagatelle to tell her she wasn't alone. We exchanged a look of complicity, and smiled at each other, perhaps to take our minds off our powerlessness in the face of the destruction of our lives. Anni smelled of rotting grass, roots and undergrowth, as if his days lying beneath the trees were a prelude to his final return to earth.

He spent half an hour upstairs. When he came down, he looked satisfied, almost serene. Could he have understood something essential during his tête-à-tête with the corpse? Without a word, he returned to Dad's side, and they began smoking again.

That night, Dad and I were sitting at the big kitchen table, when Léa, who was warming some soup for us, asked, "How old was Rudy?"

"I don't know... thirty... or thirty-one, I think," said Dad, a little nonplussed, as if he were wondering why he had never asked himself the question.

"Are you sure?" asked Léa.

"Yes... at least... wait!"

He removed his thick wallet from the back pocket of his trousers. It had been stretched out of shape by all the things he was in the habit of "keeping safe" in it. Placing it on the table in front of him, he took almost everything out, before finally extracting an official document.

"He was born in 1943. So. He was thirty-three."

"Thirty-three! Incredible!" murmured Léa.

Dad showed us Rudy's ID card, which he had kept on him since the day he had gone to get him in German Switzerland. It had been new, acquired specially for that journey, the only one in his life. Rudy's name was Rudolf Biedermann. He was born in Aarberg in the canton of Berne. He was 1.66 metres tall, and had red hair. In the photo, he was smiling openly, with the innocence of someone who has his life before him and doesn't know what lies ahead. He must have been less than twenty at the time, but his face was the one I had always known. His smile was the smile of someone who did not understand that his soul had somehow found its way into the wrong body, and that as a result he would have to live as a being apart, isolated from his fellow humans.

The next morning, a long black car entered our yard. The two funeral employees, dressed in black, exchanged words with my father, before coming into the house with a large coffin made of light-coloured wood. Dad waited for them below. When they finally emerged with Rudy, they paused and looked around them, as if they could hear solemn music playing. They remained motionless for a long minute in the midst of our silent farm. It was a way to honour him before his final departure. Then Dad got in the back of the car. He wanted to accompany Rudy on his journey to the little cemetery in Aarberg, where a place had been set aside for him in the Biedermanns' family plot.

VIII

Léa is dressed stylishly, in black stockings and a suit that strike me as unsuitable for the occasion. I stand back to let her enter. "How're things, kiddo?" she says, looking me up and down. It has always seemed to annoy Léa to have such an inhibited and self-effacing brother, who makes no effort to escape his destiny, shows no desire to stand out.

She has on that smile that is still a little foreign to me, even after years to get used to it. A permanent fixture, the smile seems less a sign of blissful enlightenment than a form of makeup, like the pencil-thin, black half-circles that have taken the place of eyebrows above her big green eyes. I often feel surprised that this is my sister, Léa, who used to complain at having knees that were too big, who deployed all sorts of strategies to avoid getting dirty, whom Dad had once called a "potato flower" because potato flowers are necessary and pretty though they never bear fruit. Léa, who has transformed herself into a woman who walks slowly in the street so that men can watch her better.

Now, standing in the centre of my orange *kilim*, she takes in my bachelor flat, which suddenly seems to have no independent existence outside her gaze. She is surprised that I'm not yet ready to leave.

We get into her car, an immense, luxurious Ford Taurus she has no doubt chosen because it can accommodate the length of her legs. On the front passenger seat, I feel as if I'm far away from her, though barely fifty centimetres separate us. This is luxury – enlarging space, broadening the horizon, giving you the sense that you count for something... I ask her how her husband and children are. She replies that her children are with their friends in the house in Grignan for two weeks' holiday, and that Grégoire is in Boston for an important conference. "Two weeks of freedom!" she adds with a wry expression. "I'm looking forward to frittering it away." Léa has succeeded in living the life that most people want to live.

She holds the steering wheel firmly with both hands, moving it with abrupt little gestures, her bracelets jingling with each small change of direction. She cranes her neck forward as she drives, as if a few extra centimetres might help her see further. She doesn't know it, but she looks just like our mother when she used to take our Toyota into town in the old days.

The car glides over the peaceful roads. On either side, graceful slopes rise and fall. In the distance, the grass in the meadows looks too green, artificial in its uniformity, as if nature has renounced its true self. We drive through several deserted villages, where the steam rising from piles of manure, sometimes stacked in front of the barns in traditional, rectangular blocks, is the only sign of life. You would have to linger awhile to discover the unseen activity beneath this tranquil surface, just as a wildlife spotter must remain long motionless and hidden, before all the little forest creatures gradually lose their timidity, and resume their normal lives.

* * *

"No, Mr. Sutter isn't here. It would be preferable if he were, of course, but his presence is not indispensable. We can go ahead with the sale perfectly well in his absence. Are you family?"

"I'm his son. And the lady with me, over there, is my sister."

Léa is standing some way behind me. The auctioneer and his sidekick glance at her, dive for a moment into the paperwork spread out in front of them, then look back at her with interest, as if needing to confirm the impression that has fleetingly excited their neurons. Léa is lost in the centre of our yard, where she hasn't set foot since the day she left to go to business school. She smiles at them, and they smile back, respectfully bowing their heads.

The legs of the bailiffs' little trestle table are wedged between our shiny round paving stones, glossy and golden-brown in the yellow light of the sun on this morning in early June. With an ache of sadness, I recognise several of the stones, their particular texture and curvature, especially one that is much darker than the others and looks like black jasper. In my childhood fancy, it had been a fragment of meteorite, lonely and out of place amidst its vulgar, terrestrial companions.

A dozen men in shirtsleeves, jackets in hand, wander through our farm between the stable, the barn and the house. The smoke of cigarettes and cigars follows their somewhat aimless meanderings; when they get together for a whispered conference, the cloud thickens, until it casts a shadow over their heads. I'm relieved that no one I know is there. There are a few Swiss Germans, some men from Berne and Fribourg, and some Frenchmen – but, out of propriety or superstition, no vulture-like neighbours.

The farm tools are exhibited along the outside wall of the barn. I recognise the barrel used to treat grapes with copper sulphate, the harvester, the muck-spreader, the milking machine, the metal posts tied into bundles, the potato planter... No one dares come too close. They all pass by at a decent distance, sizing up at a glance the condition of whatever might interest them. They almost seem afraid that one of the objects might suddenly leap at their faces.

The old Hürlimann tractor, the two wooden ploughs, the harrows, and the other large pieces of machinery are all lined up inside the barn, as if they are on parade. Without putting out their cigarettes, some buyers hurry instead into the stables, to inspect the surviving cows: two Simmentals and four red Holsteins. The vegetable garden has been abandoned, and is overrun with weeds. With nothing to keep them in check, they have grown as tall as the stakes around which our green beans once climbed.

I go into the house, hoping to find that Dad has taken refuge there. Ever since he started living alone, he has slept in the little bedroom, now empty of all its former clutter, which he has simply moved to another room. He lives only in the bedroom and the kitchen. His body is a worn-out machine whose moving parts have all seized up. His backbone is stiff and twisted, so that he walks bent almost double, as if he were constantly seated on a chair. His frozen joints make movement difficult. The slightest physical effort gives him pain, but he perseveres without complaining. His mind refuses to accept his bent body.

Half of his income comes from the sale of milk at a guaranteed price; the other half from the occasional sale of a calf, a cow, or beets at the end of the year. He also sometimes sells a few eggs to the inhabitants of the new cluster of villas built at the edge of the village. It must give them a sense of gratification to pay over the odds for these precious, elliptical shapes, and to have some contact with this blue-clad farmer who looks like the sole survivor of a remote era. It doesn't seem to matter to them that Dad barely greets them, and makes no attempt at conversation. He works ten hours a day, but it is ten hours at a loss, and all the attempts my sister and I have made in the last few years to persuade him to accept a professional restructuring of the farm have been in vain.

Dad has developed a permanent siege-like mentality. Whenever I visit, he talks about looming cataclysms, the chaotically changed climate, investors speculating wildly on turning vegetables into fuel, land abandoned by farmers and reconquered by the forest, nine billion inhabitants on a planet that is getting smaller and smaller... He is proud to continue to produce a little milk, a little meat, a little sugar. It's as if he believes that the future nourishment of the entire human race depends on small-time farmers, scattered over the surface of the globe, resisting change – and he is one of them, with his few hundred square metres of crops.

* * *

"Everything looks so pathetic!"

Léa's sudden presence at my side takes me by surprise. I glance at her shoes, which have been ruined by the rough paving stones. Red and expensive-looking, with high heels, they are now dirty and stained. For some reason, it touches me to see her tottering like this, on her heels.

"Yup."

"Everything seems smaller, don't you think?"

"Yup."

"It all looks older too."

"It's like everything's dead."

I look at her in despair. The furniture of our lives was disappearing before our very eyes.

"Are you okay?"

"Yeah."

I've never been able to hide my feelings from her. Léa doesn't believe me. She looks hard at me, as if she is trying to inject some of her own strength into my soul.

"Where's Dad?" she asks.

"Not inside, apparently."

She examines the house, window by window, then the barn, the half-open door of the shed. "What if he's lying in ambush somewhere, like a sniper?"

"Come off it."

"Some people resist," she says.

"He's probably just hiding."

"I heard a story about a farmer who left with his cows before his farm was liquidated. A farmer with his animals but no home... He wandered through the countryside for a few weeks, squatted in meadows, was taken in here or there by other farmers."

Behind us, one of the bailiffs shouts that the auction is starting. Patting their trouser pockets to confirm that the bundled wads of notes are still there, the buyers gather round to watch the proceedings. They still don't dare come too close to the little table.

"Come on," I say, taking my sister's hand.

"What?"

"Let's get out of here."

"Where are we going?"

"To the café." I give her a tug to get her moving.

"The café?"

"Dad might be there."

We take the Passage of the Bees, empty of pollen-gathering insects; then the Street of Gaiety, empty of gaiety. Léa walks slowly, teetering on the uneven village paths. Her eyes are fixed on the ground, as if she is crossing a minefield, though in fact she is only trying to avoid stepping in a cowpat. The physical effort flushes her face and covers her in a film of sweat that looks strange on her. Suddenly she seems younger, and I have the feeling she is becoming the former Léa again – the Léa who was always out of place. Do I love her? I've never really asked myself the question. Perhaps it's something brothers and sisters rarely ask themselves, or at least only if there's a problem. I wait for her, then take her arm and help her along.

"Thanks, Gus. It's so hot!"

"You're wearing far too many clothes. It is summer."

"But not like that summer... Do you...?"

Léa leans gently against me for support. An overdressed woman can be as immobile as an elderly person. Her irises seem to have distilled an essence of green from the surrounding meadows. In her gaze is a sliver of soul that is not her own, that she has inherited from our mother, and which gleams more or less intensely, depending what she is looking at. It could be the reason I feel uneasy when she stares at me too long.

In the café, there are only three customers. They are seated at a single table, but a good distance apart on the benches, giving the impression that they don't know each other. As if tied to an invisible wire, they raise their heads simultaneously to look at the newcomers. I recognise Grin and Pellaux, a little greyer with the years but otherwise unchanged. I don't greet them because they don't greet me. They can't take their eyes off Léa, and begin to whisper amongst themselves. They seem astounded to discover that Time, which drags their own monotonous existences implacably towards oblivion, is not always so cruel, and can transform a simple village girl into a woman of the sort who appears on TV or in magazines.

"I don't believe it! Gus!"

"Hi, Maddie."

She sets her cigarette down in an ashtray behind the counter, and comes towards us.

"Madame!" she says, by way of a greeting to my sister, then turns her full attention to me.

"Gus! Gus! It's so good to see you."

She takes firm hold of me, to kiss me on both cheeks. Maddie has been a waitress at the Bellevue ever since she left school at sixteen. Her eyes are magnified by the thick lenses of her glasses. She gives me a knowing smile, as if trying to draw me back to the times when we would wander through the village together on rainy days. The times when we would gather up snails – from under leaves, from hedges and walls – to place them side by side. "It's just that they move so slowly on their own," Maddie would say, convinced that it was our duty to facilitate their trysts. And, in fact, they would end up mounting each other, joining their long sticky feet together like suction cups, in twos, threes or fours, merging into piles of soft flesh that we watched as though they were orgies.

Maddie has never left the village. No one has come to whisk her away. The café's silent customers are her only company.

"Are you looking for your father?"

"Yeah."

"You've just missed him."

She points to a table in a corner under the dusty showcase displaying the trophies of the shooting club. A half-litre carafe and a glass testify to his presence.

"Damn."

"He was drinking white wine all afternoon. You know... about the auction... I'm sorry."

"Me too, but that's how it is."

"Yeah. That's life."

"Do you know where he went?"

"No. He didn't say a word the whole time he was here... Can I get you both something to drink?"

"I think I might know..."

"A lemonade, perhaps?"

"The round field! He must be there."

"A coke?"

"Nothing for me, thanks," says Léa.

"Come on! At least drink a glass of water before you leave."

"No, thanks."

"How about you, Gus?"

"Okay. Quickly."

She moves behind the counter with surprising agility, like an acrobat after years of repeating the same moves, and fills a large glass from the tap. She hands it to me, then stays close to make sure I drink the clear, cool water she has offered. As I bring the glass to my lips, her face takes on a mischievous expression.

"It's fine to drink. It's village water," she says.

I swallow a mouthful.

"It comes from the reservoir..."

I swallow another mouthful.

"No one swims there anymore."

I swallow a final mouthful, looking Maddie straight in the eyes. Under the too-tight, shiny black dress, the flesh-coloured stockings, the low-necked, slightly-too-thin white blouse that lets her bra show through, there is so much flesh, so much accumulated fat, that is not really part of her, but is a shroud that has gradually enveloped her, the product of a stubborn and endless boredom, an invisible and silent unhappiness, falling slowly and unobtrusively, from morning to evening, like warm summer rain. The lithe, strong body of the little animal I once knew and loved has disappeared.

"Thanks."

A veil passes over her eyes.

"I think I know where he is," I said.

"Your father?"

"Yeah. He must be in the round field. You know... the big maples."

"You could be right."

"We'll go and look."

Léa, impatient to get away, nods her agreement. As I hold the door for my sister, I meet the gaze of the little trapped animal, who smoothes down her dress, holding back tears. I remember the days of my own depression.

We cross the fields. Under the fierce sun, the last scraps of fog are drifting towards the outer edge of the forest. The path consists of slabs of white concrete, held together by black asphalt, which contracts in the winter with the frost and expands in the summer with the heat. They look like the pieces of an immense domino game, whose dots have been erased by time.

"We won't be able to avoid selling the buildings and the farm and all the land," says Léa.

I don't reply.

"According to Grégoire, it's worth a million, a million and a half. He says these properties are in demand these days. It's not so far from town, and with a little refurbishment..."

"We can't. Dad would never agree."

"Would you rather wait until he's forced to have another auction? If we did that, the price would go down. Look, with the money, we could buy him a flat in the village, in the new neighbourhood..."

"Stop! Shut up! Just think about what you're saying."

"Listen, Gus! We have to be realistic. Dad won't be able to go on for long. It's finished. And with the money that's left over, you... Well, it seems to me that you could use it, couldn't you?"

I stop walking, and look at Léa.

"That's not the problem."

"What do you mean? Yes, it's a problem."

"I don't need that money. And you're getting on my nerves."

"There's no other way. You don't live in the real world, Gus."

"You don't live in our world, that's for sure."

"Oh, come on!"

Her distressed face glows. She's strangely flushed. I don't think I've ever seen her looking so foreign. The problem is that we didn't have the same childhood.

The meadows are in a state of utter disorder. They have been overrun by fescue grass, a plant scorned even by animals, which will eat it only as a last resort, and take days to digest it. Not a trace of alfalfa or cock's-foot remains. The lush, green hay-grass and the clover have gone, suffocated by more aggressive species of grass and dandelions. Along the side of the path, where the earth is crumbly, blue sage and rust-coloured sorrel are growing.

"We're there," says Léa.

"Yeah."

There seems to be a tacit agreement between us that we should be able to find our father without calling his name. We hear a high-pitched, whirring sound behind us. Two cyclists, like multi-coloured beetles in their carapace-like gear, are heading in our direction. They stop alongside us.

"Hello. Do you know where the cyclocross track is?"

"No."

"Oh. Strange. We thought..."

"*No.*"

They push their feet back into the tight pedal-straps. As they set off, I shout "idiots!" but they pretend not to hear.

"Gus! Look!"

Léa gestures towards a narrow strip of trodden grass. Tracks lead to the slope next to the big maples, where Dad is seated on the ground. His head and shoulders are concealed by the tall grass. His thick, chestnut-coloured velour jacket is speckled with yellow pollen seeds. Sensing our presence behind him, he trembles, but he doesn't turn around. Neither does he look at me, when I sit down wordlessly next to him. Léa, who has followed me after a short delay, takes a cloth handkerchief out of her handbag and unfolds it on Dad's other side, before sitting on it. We all stare at the same imaginary point, beyond the dark barrier of the woods below, which barely hide the new villas.

We stay there for a long time, staring into the dusty, early-summer light, trying to make ourselves a little absent, to find in the distance something solid and definite, despite our splintered lives. I know for sure that we will never talk about this tenuous, shared moment.

We are sitting in the exact spot where Bagatelle died, struck by lightning during the storm that destroyed the hen-house. It had been a few days before we remembered where she was, with her strange, sudden determination never to move again. We'd found her lying with all four legs in the air, animated one last time from head to hoof by a massive electric current, connected for a fraction of a second to the power of the cosmos.

Dad had got out of the tractor first, followed by Sheriff. With his muzzle to the ground and his eyes raised to sky, our dog described a wide circle around the swollen corpse, emitting long whines, not daring to approach. Bagatelle's belly was swollen by gas, making her limbs look like ridiculous appendages. Flies came and went freely from all her orifices, lingering over the wettest parts. They seemed to delight especially in the blue tongue that showed between her pulled-back lips and her limp lower jaw.

"She must have been toasted on the spot!" said Dad.

We had to hurry to hoist her up to the road in time to meet the slaughterhouse truck. Dad unrolled the rope attached to the hook on the back of the tractor, tied Bagatelle's forelegs together in a noose, and climbed back into the driver's seat. The engine and the immense carcass juddered to life at the same time. Falling sideways in a black tornado of flies, Bagatelle was dragged wretchedly along behind the big wheels, ploughing one last furrow in the waterlogged earth. On the road, we waited together in silence for half an hour. Sheriff, pressing himself against us with his tail between his legs, was inconsolable. From time to time, Dad gave him a pat, but his heart wasn't in it.

The truck, with its steel-jawed crane attachment, drew up alongside us. The man from the slaughterhouse greeted us from his window, before turning off his engine and climbing down. He looked at Bagatelle's remains.

"How did she die?" he asked Dad, as if it had some bearing on the job ahead.

"Lightning."

"Eugh."

They didn't exchange another word. Their only meetings had been when an animal had died, circumstances not conducive to the growth of cordial relations. We watched the manoeuvrings of the articulated arm. The metal claws opened above Bagatelle, then dropped to close around her and lift her up. Suddenly, all her valves opened, releasing the gases that had built up in her stomach. The instant the pestilential stench reached us, I had to run off to vomit. Sheriff raced off in a dead straight line, until he disappeared around the bend in the road. With a hand in front of his nose, Dad alone remained stoic in the midst of the flies, which flew in ever more frenzied acrobatic formations through the vapours that, for them, must have been what we humans call an earthly paradise.

*   *   *

After a long silence seated on the grass between his son and his daughter, Dad gave a brief, harsh grunt, as if he had finally discovered the consolation he had been seeking in the recesses of his being. I thought then that he would have liked at that very moment to be absorbed by the earth, swallowed gently into the depths, in order, at last, to merge with the relics of all the men and women who had been nourished by these once fertile lands.